BIG NATE

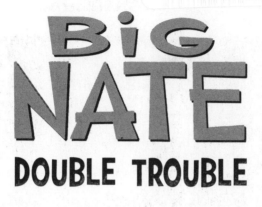

DOUBLE TROUBLE

ALSO BY LINCOLN PEIRCE

Big Nate on a Roll
Big Nate Goes for Broke
Big Nate Flips Out
Big Nate: In the Zone
Big Nate Lives It Up
Big Nate Blasts Off

Big Nate: What Could Possibly Go Wrong?
Big Nate: Here Goes Nothing
Big Nate: Genius Mode
Big Nate: Mr. Popularity

Big Nate Boredom Buster
Big Nate Fun Blaster
Big Nate Doodlepalooza
Big Nate Laugh-O-Rama
Big Nate Super Scribbler
Big Nate Puzzlemania

Lincoln Peirce

BiG NATE
DOUBLE TROUBLE

BALZER + BRAY
An Imprint of HarperCollins*Publishers*

ISBN 978-0-06-283946-6

Typography by Sasha Illingworth
18 19 20 21 22   CG/LSCH   10 9 8 7 6 5 4 3 2 1
❖
First Edition

BiG NATE

DOUBLE TROUBLE

Lincoln Peirce

IN A CLASS BY HIMSELF

For Jessica

CHAPTER 1

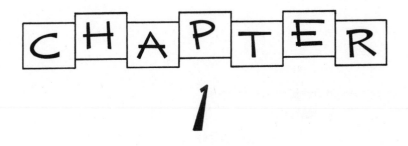

She could have called on anybody.

There were twenty-two other kids in the classroom, and they all had their hands in the air. Francis did. Teddy did. Gina did, of course. Even Nick Blonsky, who usually sits in the back row with his pencil up his nose, had his hand raised. She could have called on one of them, right?

Guess who she calls on.

Mrs. Godfrey always does this. She always calls on me when I don't know the answer. And she can TELL I don't know it. Ever hear somebody say that dogs can smell fear? That's Mrs. Godfrey. She's like a dog.

A big, ugly, nasty dog.

I sort of skooch down in my seat. The whole class is staring at me. My ears start to burn, then my cheeks. I can feel tiny droplets of sweat beading up on my forehead.

○ ° ○ ○ ○ ° ° ○ ○ ° ○ ° ○ ° ○ ° ○ ○ ○ ° ° ○ ° ○ ° ° ° ° ○ ° ○ ° ° ○

"WELL?" she barks.

I've heard that on an average day, you use about 10 percent of your brainpower. Well, sitting here with my mouth turning as dry as a sack of sand, I really need that other 90 percent to kick in. But my mind is blank.

Mrs. Godfrey steps away from the chalkboard and starts toward me. She looks mad. No, worse than mad. She looks mean. Her face is flushed. I can see tiny flecks of spittle at the corners of her mouth. That's pretty gross. I brace myself. . . .

And then the bell rings!

And rings. And keeps on ringing. Except it doesn't really sound like the school bell. It sounds more like . . .

I was DREAMING!! I blink hard, then let out a huge sigh of relief. I've never been so happy to hear that alarm clock in my entire life. Not that I'm ready to get up or anything. Closing my eyes again, I flop back down onto my pillow. ZZZZZZ . . .

Hey, thanks a lot, Dad. Way to break it to me gently. Nice parenting.

Actually, his parenting skills aren't that bad. He makes the nastiest tuna casserole you've ever tasted, but he's pretty harmless—especially compared to some of the psycho dads I've seen at Little League games. It's just that Dad's kind of clueless. He has no idea what it's like to be me.

PARENTAL FACT: *Once you go bald, you completely lose your ability to relate to anyone under the age of 30.*

I mean, how long has it been since he was in middle school—thirty or forty years? I think he's forgotten how it feels to be held prisoner all day long in a building that smells like a combination of chalk dust, ammonia, and mystery meat. He can't remember what it's like to be an average sixth grader.

YAWNN...

zZZZIP!

Not that I'm an average sixth grader. Okay, I'll admit that I'm not exactly Joe Honor Roll, but answer me this: When I get out there in the real world, is anybody

going to care whether or not I know who was vice president under Warren G. Harding? (And don't try to pretend that YOU know who it was, because you don't.) The point is, I want to use my talents for more than just memorizing useless facts. I'm meant for bigger things. I am . . .

DESTINED FOR GREATNESS!

I'm still not 100 percent sure what KIND of greatness I'm destined for, but I'll figure it out. I've got options. I keep a list on my closet door about this very subject.

There's also stuff I definitely WON'T achieve greatness in, like opera, synchronized swimming, and cat grooming. Enough said.

Let's get back to the unfortunate fact that today's a school day. But what KIND? You know, not all school days are created equal. You can rank them by category. (Just so you know, I'm really into ranking stuff. One time I spent a solid week ranking every kind of snack food I could think of. At the top: Cheez Doodles. At the bottom: rice cakes.)

DAD FACT:
Dad handed out rice cakes for Halloween one year. That was also the year our house got egged. Connect the dots, Dad.

If I were to grade the different kinds of school days report-card style, here's how they'd stack up:

A+ FIELD TRIP DAYS

I'm not talking about lame field trips, when a teacher makes you walk around the neighborhood on Earth Day picking up trash. I'm talking about an all-day get-on-a-bus-and-go-somewhere field trip. Even if they give you

a work sheet in the hope that you might actually learn something, you can usually come up with an excuse not to do it. That's what I did last year when we went to the aquarium.

B SPECIAL EVENTS DAYS

This is when classroom time gets eaten up by something better, like a movie or an assembly. Or, better yet, some sort of emergency. Last spring, Mrs. Czerwicki's wig caught on fire and set off

the smoke alarm in the faculty lounge. We got to evacuate the building and ended up playing ultimate Frisbee on the lawn for an hour. That was awesome. For everybody except Mrs. Czerwicki.

C- SUBSTITUTE TEACHER DAYS

I think we can all agree that subs are almost always better than the real teachers. By "better" I mean "more clueless." The absolute best subs are the fresh-out-of-college ones who have never taught a day in their lives. Frankly, they're not very bright. Or maybe they're just really gullible.

D NORMAL DAYS

Unfortunately, most days are like this: You spend six-and-a-half action-packed hours studying subjects like photosynthesis and the War of 1812. Thrilling. You get home after school and your parents are like:

And you think about it for a solid ten seconds, and then you say:

F TRAIN WRECKS

There are so many ways for a school day to go wrong that it's almost impossible to list them

all. You could get screamed at by a teacher (usually Mrs. Godfrey) for absolutely no reason, which seems to happen to me a lot. You could get roughed up by Chester, the school bully who looks like he spikes his chocolate milk with human growth hormone. Or your teacher could nail you with a quiz or a test you never saw coming. . . .

Now there's a horrifying thought. Do we have a test today? I don't remember any teacher mentioning a test yesterday. But, like I already told you, I don't remember much of anything they say. I usually start to lose interest right around the time I hear:

SETTLE DOWN, CLASS.

("Settle down, class," in teacher speak, means "Let the mind-numbing boredom begin.")

YAK YAK YAK YAK YAK YAK YAK YAK
YAK YAK YAK YAK YAK YAK YAK
YAK YAK YAK YAK YAK YAK
YAK YAK YAK YAK YAK YAK
AND BY THE WAY THERE'S
A TEST TOMORROW YAK
YAK YAK YAK YAK YAK
YAK YAK YAK YAK YAK
YAK YAK YAK YAK YAK YAK
YAK YAK YAK YAK YAK
YAK YAK YAK YAK YAK

It's times like this I wish I paid better attention in class. Like Francis.

Francis!!! HE'LL know whether or not we have a test today!

APPLE, CELERY, SANDWICH, YOGURT!

Here's the thing about Francis: He knows just about everything. He's always got his nose buried in the "Book of Facts," and he takes school pretty seriously. The truth is, he's kind of a geek. But I'm allowed to call him that because we're tight. We've known each other since the first day of kindergarten, when he started snoring during nap time. So I hit him in the head with my Thomas the Tank Engine lunch box, and we've been best friends ever since.

Let me see if he's up yet.

Yup, he's up. And he's reading, of course.

But . . . wait a minute! Look what he's reading!

So we MUST have a test today!!

This is bad. This is VERY bad. First, because my social studies textbook is in my locker at school.

And second, because I'm suddenly remembering what Mrs. Godfrey said to me after our LAST test:

IF YOU DO THIS POORLY ON THE **NEXT** TEST, NATE, YOU COULD VERY WELL END UP IN **SUMMER SCHOOL!**

Yipe. We've got social studies first period. That only gives me about forty-five minutes to study my class notes.

CLASS NOTES... CLASS NOTES...

WHERE ARE MY CLASS NOTES?

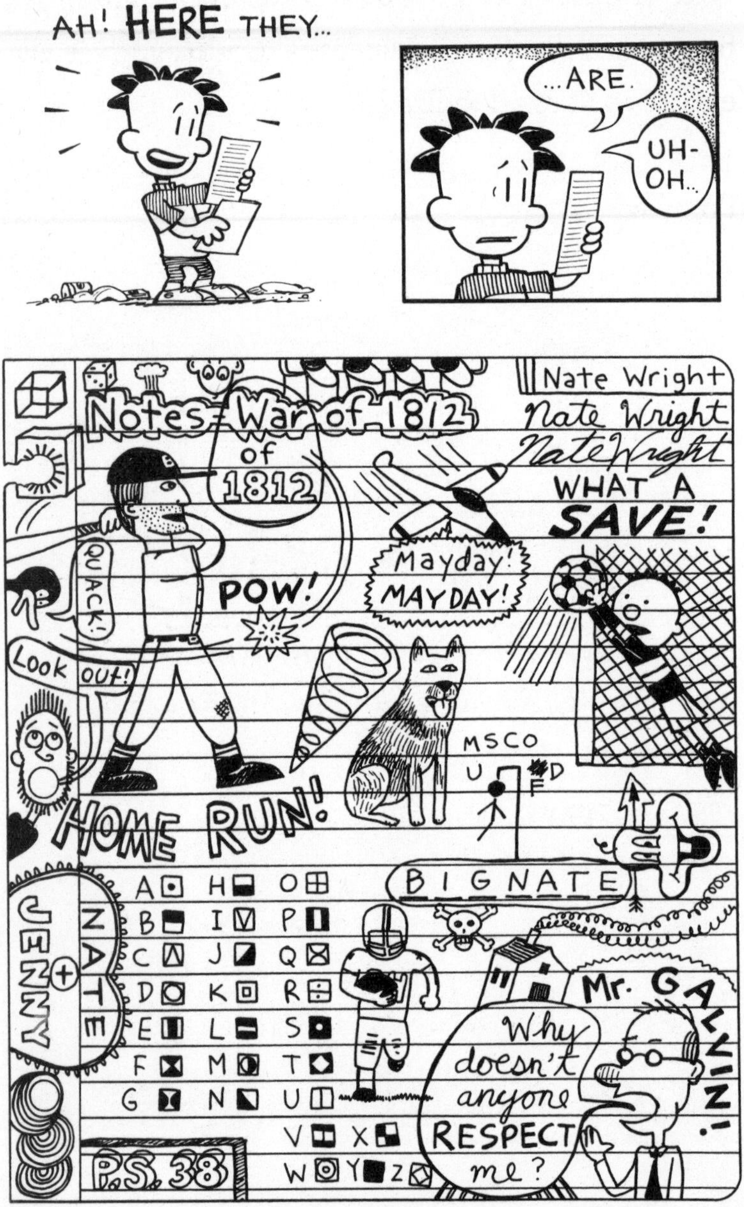
AH! HERE THEY...
...ARE.
UH-OH...
Notes: War of 1812
of 1812
Nate Wright
Nate Wright
Nate Wright
WHAT A SAVE!
QUACK!
POW!
Mayday! MAYDAY!
Look out!
MSCO
HOME RUN!
BIGNATE
NATE + JENNY
P.S. 38
Mr. GALVIN!
Why doesn't anyone RESPECT me?

Well, it looks like my class notes aren't going to be much help. Not unless Mrs. Godfrey gives us extra credit for doodling.

I'm dead.

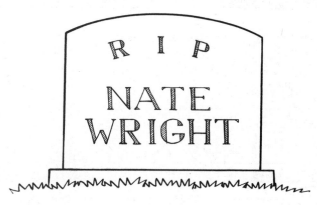

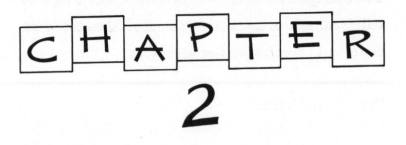

CHAPTER 2

"Breakfast is the most important meal of the day."

Have you ever noticed that's what people always say right before they stick a bowl of lumpy oatmeal in your face?

Now Dad's rambling on about how a high-fiber diet changed his life, but I'm barely listening. I'm still freaked out about this social studies test that could land me in summer school.

"Summer." "School."

Talk about two words that don't go together. Sort of like "oat" and "meal."

Actually, I have no idea what summer school is even like. Francis thinks it's probably just like regular school, only hotter.

But other kids say that in summer school, the teachers make you work. And they're not talking about work sheets or chapter reviews. It's more like scraping gum off desks or scrubbing the toilets in the boys' locker room (which I hope isn't true, because those toilets are totally disgusting). It sounds pretty bad.

...AND AFTER THIS, MY CAR NEEDS WASHING!

The only kid I know who's ever gone to summer school is Chester. I guess I could ask him what it's like. Except the last time I tried to ask Chester something, he stuffed me into a garbage can. He's kind of a psycho.

KEEP OUR SCHOOL CLEAN

ALL I ASKED WAS "CAN I BORROW A PENCIL?"

Whatever. The point is, summer school can't be good. I can't think of anything nastier.

Suddenly, right on cue . . . *IN WALKS ELLEN.*

Okay, I CAN think of something—someONE— nastier. Summer school only lasts eight weeks. A fifteen-year-old sister is forever. Until she turns sixteen, which is probably even worse.

Me and Ellen

Sisters don't have to be teenagers to be obnoxious, though. They're pretty much born that way.

If you have an older sister, you know exactly what I mean. You've been there. You feel my pain. If you DON'T have an older sister, congratulations. And welcome to my nightmare.

ELLEN FACT:
Every few months, she decides she doesn't like the way she laughs, so she changes it.

HA HA HA!... NO, THAT'S NOT RIGHT...

TOP 5 MOST ANNOYING THINGS ABOUT ELLEN!

5.) She is constantly begging Dad to buy her a cat.

We'll name her "Miss Kissy-kins"!

annoying → MORE annoying → MOST ANNOYING!!

4.

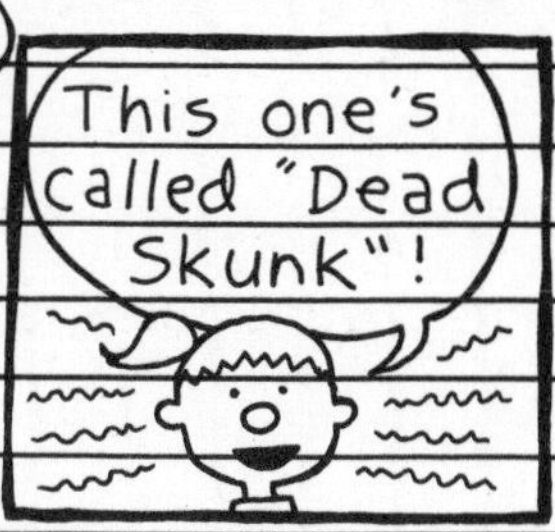
This one's called "Dead Skunk"!

She wears perfume that makes her smell like a gift shop full of scented candles.

3. She got a karaoke machine for her 12th birthday, and she still hasn't outgrown it.

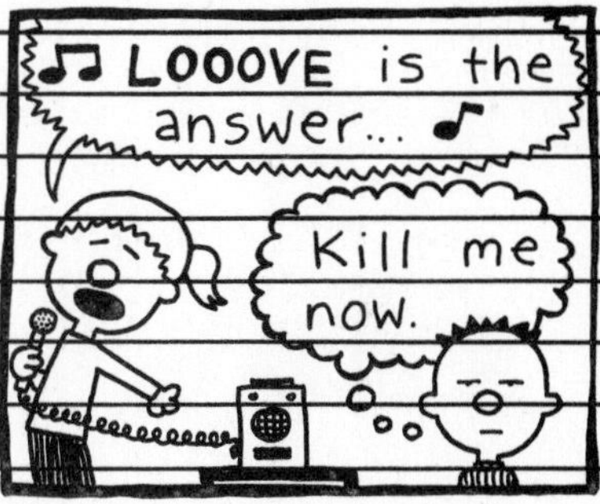
♫ LOOOVE is the answer... ♪
Kill me now.

2.

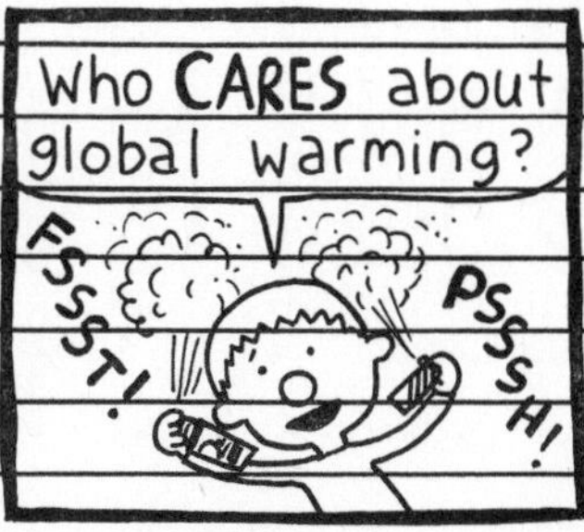
Who CARES about global warming?
FSSST!
PSSSH!

All her hair care products are single-handedly destroying the ozone layer.

1. NOBODY except me realizes how completely OBNOXIOUS she is.

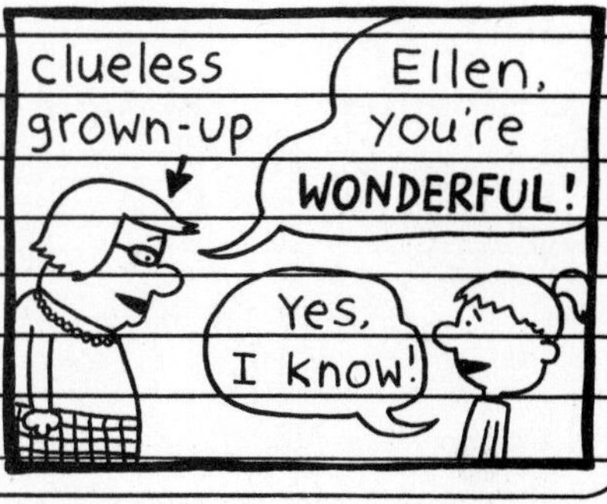
clueless grown-up
Ellen, you're WONDERFUL!
Yes, I know!

You want to know what else is annoying about Ellen? She doesn't have these types of problems. She's never had to worry about summer school, because she's always been a good student. Which I get reminded of practically every day.

WHY CAN'T YOU BE MORE LIKE YOUR SISTER?

Right, like that's my goal in life: to be more like a high school cheerleader. Thanks, but no thanks.

Huh? Oh. Dad's talking again.

Note to self: Add "you can't shut her up" to list of annoying things about Ellen.

Hm. Don't think Dad really bought that. He's giving me "the Look."

THE LOOK
*Level One
on Dad's sus-
picion meter.
It means
he's not really
sure you're
being straight
with him.*

THE SQUINT
*Level Two
is basically
Dad's way of
saying, "You
can't possibly
be serious."*

**THE HAIRY
EYEBALL**
*Level Three
When Dad drops
a Hairy Eyeball
on you, look out.
Prepare for him
to go ballistic.*

Dad's only at Level One right now, but I can see where this is going. So I'd better get out of here before he asks any more questions.

ZOOM !

Whew! That was close. He has no idea I could end up in summer school.

Not unless he and Mrs. Godfrey are having secret, late-night phone conversations.

EW. TIME TO THINK ABOUT SOMETHING ELSE.

Nice spot for a nap, Spitsy. Shouldn't you be off chasing squirrels or something?

Spitsy belongs to Mr. Eustis, who lives next door. And, in case the doofy-looking dog sweater and giant funnel on his head didn't tip you off, Spitsy

is the ultimate dog nerd. He's afraid of mailmen. He eats his own poop. And don't try throwing him a tennis ball. I did that once and we ended up at the animal hospital getting his stomach pumped. It's a long story.

But I don't want to rag on Spitsy. Spitsy's okay. After all, he's a dog, and all dogs are cool in my book. Except maybe those freaky little hairless Chihuahuas.

SPITSY FACT:
He has a crush on Francis's cat, Pickles.

It must be nice to be you, Spitsy. You get to hang out all day, sleeping in the sun. You don't have to worry about Hairy Eyeballs. Or big sisters. Or teachers.

WAIT a minute! Maybe *I* don't have to worry about the test either!

What if I can get out of it?

What if I can convince Mrs. Godfrey to let me take the test tomorrow instead of today? Then I'll borrow Francis's class notes and cram for twenty-four hours. That'll at least give me a CHANCE to pass the stupid thing.

See, that's why dogs are so much better than cats. Cats never help you do ANYTHING. They just lie around the house, scratching up the furniture and licking themselves.

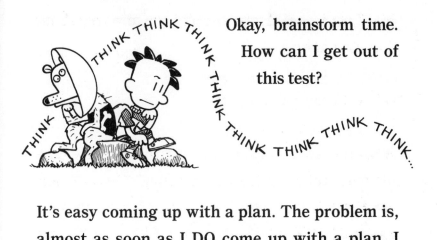

Okay, brainstorm time. How can I get out of this test?

It's easy coming up with a plan. The problem is, almost as soon as I DO come up with a plan, I think of a reason it won't work.

PLAN A: ILLNESS

As soon as the test starts, I hold my breath until my face turns all red. Then I tell Mrs. Godfrey I feel really, really sick.

WHY IT WON'T WORK

She keeps a thermometer in her desk.

JUST AS I THOUGHT: 98.6°!

PLAN B: INJURY

I wrap my hand in bandages, then tell her I can't write because I sprained my wrist.

WHY IT WON'T WORK

She'll make me take the test left-handed. Yup, she's that mean.

PLAN C: TRAGIC ACCIDENT

I pretend to hit my head against the door on my way into the classroom, then act like I've got amnesia.

WHY IT WON'T WORK

I used that one two weeks ago.

PLAN D: THE TRUTH

I walk right up to Mrs. Godfrey, look her in the eye, and tell her that I didn't know there was a test today.

WHY IT WON'T WORK

The woman hates me.

Shoot. This is getting me nowhere. I've only got twenty-five minutes until the test. Twenty-five minutes until Mrs. Godfrey brings down the summer school hammer on me.

I glance at my watch. Now it's twenty-FOUR minutes. Yikes.

It's beginning to look like the only way I'll be able
to avoid this test is . . . is . . .

. . . is to skip school altogether!

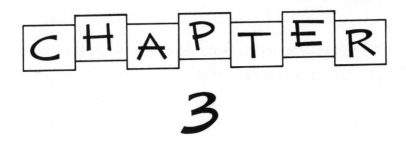

CHAPTER 3

Yes! That's it! I'll skip school! I'll take the day off! I'll pretend somebody just invented a new holiday!

I'll stop right here.

What am I DOING? Nobody gets away with skipping school at P.S. 38. It's impossible.

Why? Two words: "THE MACHINE."

Not a REAL machine, like that funky-looking thing the janitor uses to buff up the floors. The Machine isn't something you can see or touch. But it's there.

The Machine watches you. It knows your every move. And if you're not where you're supposed to be, the Machine tracks you down. Here's how:

1. THE SEATING CHART
Teachers always tell you where to sit. They claim it helps them remember kids' names. Right. Like they care what our names are.

They REALLY do it to keep tabs on you. One look at the chart and they know right away if you're not at your desk. Then the Machine starts up.

2. THE ATTENDANCE SHEET

Teachers write everything down. Who knows why.

They fill out an attendance sheet in every class. If you're missing, a big red "X" goes next to your name. Congratulations. You're absent.

3. THE CLASSROOM HELPER

We saw a movie about bees in science. This big fat queen bee sat around the hive doing nothing while the little drones did all the work. Sound familiar?

Teachers are the queen bees. Guess who the drones are.

It's always a suck-up like Gina who volunteers, because she's so desperate to earn extra credit. Good for you, Gina. I'm sure your career as a sixth-grade classroom helper will get you into some fancy-pants college.

TAKE THIS ATTENDANCE SHEET TO THE FRONT OFFICE.

The front office. The engine that runs the Machine. And right in the middle of it is . . .

4. THE SCHOOL SECRETARY

Mrs. Shipulski's not so bad. It isn't HER fault they make her keep track of attendance. (I also don't blame her for all the times she says, "Nate, the principal will see you now.")

She's fast for an old lady. She looks over all those attendance sheets in no time. The second she spots that red "X" next to your name, she's on the phone to your parents.

There. You see how the Machine works? See how efficient it is? You can't win. There's no way to beat it.

That's my predicament. If I run off to the woods to hang out with Spitsy, it'll take about five minutes for Mrs. Shipulski to fire up the Dad hotline. Then summer school would be the LEAST of my problems. I'd probably get suspended. Or expelled. Maybe shipped to some military academy where they slap a uniform on you, give you a buzz cut, and make you say "sir" at the end of every sentence.

That settles it.

Skipping school is out. I need to be a little more creative about this. What I need is an excused absence.

An excused absence means you go to school just like normal, but you've got a parent note saying that you need to be somewhere else at a certain time. Bingo. You're free. Yesterday, Alan Olquist left halfway through science because he had to go get a wart zapped. How lucky can you get?

So all I need to do is stroll into social studies with a note from Dad saying I've got an excuse—let's say a dentist appointment—and I'm off the hook. Genius!

Yeah, yeah. I know what you're thinking. I don't have a note from Dad. But I can take care of that.

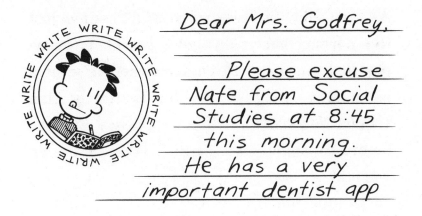

Dear Mrs. Godfrey,

Please excuse Nate from Social Studies at 8:45 this morning. He has a very important dentist app

Whoa. Nope, that won't cut it. That looks too much like my handwriting. Mrs. Godfrey will sniff that out right away. She may be loud and nasty, but the woman's not stupid.

I've got to make it look more like a grown-up's handwriting. Like DAD's. And his is wicked messy.

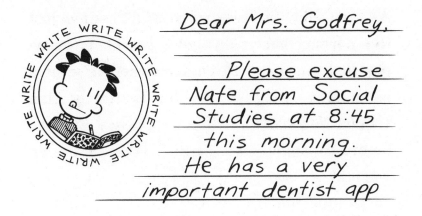

Whoops. Not THAT messy. Even *I* can't read that.

This is tougher than I thought it would be. And I'm running out of time.

Dear Mrs. Godfrey,
Please excuse Nate from
Social Studies at 8:45 this
morning. He has a very
important dentist appointment.

Hey, HEY! THAT looks like the real thing! Pretty convincing!

Hello, excused absence! Good-bye, social studies test! All that's left to do is forge Dad's signature.

Uhhhh . . . Let me think about this for a sec. Forge. Forgery. Yikes.

Isn't forgery, like, a CRIME? Don't people get thrown in JAIL for signing the wrong name on a check or for using somebody else's credit card?

Listen, I'm no Goody Two-shoes. There's a desk in the detention room with my name on it—literally. But I'm not breaking the LAW. I don't want to get dragged out of P.S. 38 in handcuffs.

This might not be such a great idea. Maybe I should just rip this thing up before somebody comes along and . . .

Oh, man. It's only Francis.

That's the downside of living next door to your best friend. He's always sneaking up behind you and invading your privacy. Not that I have anything to hide.

Okay, so I've got one tiny little thing to hide.

"Nothing?" he asks.

"Nothing," I shoot back.

"It doesn't LOOK like nothing."

Why is he acting all Sherlock Holmes on me?

I WAS FORGING AN EXCUSE NOTE... ...TO GET OUT OF TODAY'S SOCIAL STUDIES TEST.

Hmmm. Long, awkward pause. Francis has a weird expression on his face. One of those half-smiling, half-confused looks. He's either judging me for what I just told him, or he's about to fart.

"What social studies test?" he says.

Francis can be such a moron. (I've got to remind myself sometimes how smart he is.)

"The test I saw you STUDYING for this morning!"

"I wasn't studying for a test!" he says.

"Then why were you reading your social studies textbook?"

"Because I enjoy improving my mind!"

I'm going to ignore the incredibly lame statement Francis just made and focus on what he said right BEFORE that.

So . . . there's no social studies test?

THERE'S **DEFINITELY** NOT A TEST! I SH KNOW, BECAUSE I WRITE DOW YTHING SHE SAYS! IF WE VE A TEST, I WOULD HAVE N IT WHEN I WAS REVIEWING MY N BLAH BLAH BLAH BLAH BLAH BLA LAH BLAH BLAH BLAB BLAB BL B BLAB BLAB BLAH BLAH R LAH BLAH BLAH BLAB BLAB B BLAB BLAB.....

Yes! . . . YES!! . . .

"Actually," Francis says, his eyes getting all dreamy, "I sort of wish we WERE having a test today."

Sorry, Francis. But when you start acting like the mayor of Geek City, it's my job to knock some sense into you. You're lucky I didn't nail you with a heavier book.

There's the first bell. Not exactly music to my ears, but that sick feeling in the pit of my stomach is gone. No test! No summer school! This could end up being a half-decent day after all!

Yup, things are definitely looking up.

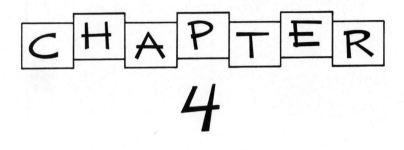

CHAPTER 4

"Hey, Nate! Taking a nap?"

OR ARE YOU DOING THE WORLD'S SLOWEST PUSH-UP?

That's Teddy. Just ignore his lame jokes. I always do.

Teddy's my OTHER best friend. Francis is #1, because I've known him longer. But Teddy is definitely #1A. He's awesome.

TEDDY FACT:
He taught me how to say "Mrs. Godfrey is fat" in Spanish.

¡SEÑORA GODFREY ES GRASA! ¡SÍ!

I wasn't so sure about him at first. That's the way it is with new kids. You sort of check them out from a distance to see if they seem cool or not. You don't want to be all Joe Friendly to them right away, because what if they turn out to be total losers?

Would you like to see my nasal spray collection?

Okay.

What am I SAYING?

random new kid →

← me

With Teddy, it was tough to tell. On his first day at P.S. 38, Principal Nichols asked me to show him around the school. Teddy was all quiet and serious. He barely said a word the whole day. I've told Teddy plenty of times since then that he seemed like a total dork.

Then he and I were paired up for a science lab. We were supposed to dissect a squid.

We were about five minutes into it when Teddy picked up our squid and pretended it was a giant booger.

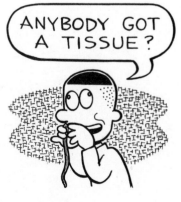

It was hilarious. I started laughing . . .

. . . and then Teddy cracked
up, too. That was the first
time I'd ever heard him
laugh. He sounded
like some sort of
crazed llama.

Oh, man. We lost it. We were laughing so hard
that we dropped our squid on the floor. Then
Mary Ellen Popowski stepped on it, which made
us laugh even harder.

That's when Mr. Galvin saw what was going on.
Wow, was he mad. He went Full Godfrey on us.

GLOSSARY
When a teacher completely snaps and starts screaming, it's called a Full Godfrey. (When Mrs. Godfrey does it, it's called Monday.)

He made us clean the squid guts off the floor. We apologized to Mary Ellen, but I guess we didn't sound sorry enough, because she kept whining that her shoes smelled like dead squid. I said maybe that was an improvement over how they smelled before.

Then I had to apologize to Mary Ellen AGAIN.

We had detention for two whole weeks.

You get in trouble that bad with somebody, and it changes the way you think about him. When I saw Teddy dangling that squid from his nose, I figured he was okay. And after we did all those detentions together, I knew we were going to be friends for life.

But that doesn't mean I'm going to let him beat me
to the flagpole!

Ha! My turbospeed is taking over!

Holy cow!! Principal Nichols!

This could get ugly. Principal Nichols is Mr. Discipline. He doesn't stand for any horsing around. And here I am body slamming him on his way into the building. Stand back. He's about to explode.

Like I was saying: Principal Nichols—what a great guy!

"Are you all right?" he asks.

"Yeah. It didn't hurt," I tell him. "You're sort of like a giant air bag."

I'll just stop talking now.

"Move along, son," says Principal Nichols, looking like "son" is the last thing he wants to call me.

Whew. Sure, I'll be happy to move along. I thought he was going to hit me with a detention for sure.

"Come on, guys," says Francis. "Only a couple minutes 'til homeroom."

I have sort of an organization problem. One of these days I really need to clean out my locker. With a dump truck. Or maybe a match.

But no time for that now. Let's see here . . . where's my lunch?

"I ran out of the house so fast this morning, I forgot to stick my lunch in my backpack!" I groan.

"No problem," Teddy tells me. "I've got you covered."

"You do?" I ask.

"Yup!" he says. "We went out for Chinese food last night. I've got a ton of leftovers."

Hm. A fortune cookie.

I like getting my fortune told. I'm way into horoscopes and Magic 8 Balls and stuff like that.

(By the way, I'm a Scorpio. That means I'm dynamic, loyal, and chock-full of animal magnetism. In other words, I rock.)

But fortune cookies bug me sometimes. Fortune-telling means predicting the future, right? But half the time, fortune cookies don't tell you ANYTHING about the future. They're just lame sayings.

Sometimes they're boring.

A large life is a series of small events.

Sometimes they're stupid.

Hair today, gone tomorrow.

CRUNCH CRUNCH

PLUS, THE COOKIES TASTE LIKE STYROFOAM.

Sometimes, like that time Dad took me and Ellen to Pu-Pu Panda, they make absolutely no sense. That one was so bizarre, I drew a comic about it:

I guess you could say I've got a love-hate relationship with fortune cookies. I hardly ever get a good one, but I still can't resist cracking 'em open.

Now THAT'S what I call a FORTUNE!

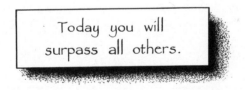

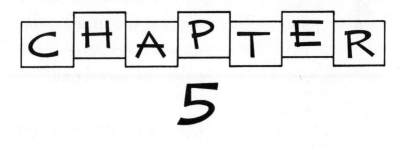

CHAPTER 5

I'm in an awesome mood when I walk into home-room. Not because of homeroom. Only a total geek would get all pumped about that.

HOMEROOM IS MY FAVORITE PART OF THE DAY!

See?

It's my FORTUNE that's great. It looked like today was going to stink out loud, and now everything's completely turned around!

"What are YOU so happy about?" Francis asks.

"I just got some amazing news," I tell him. "Have you ever heard me say I'm destined for greatness?"

"You may have mentioned it once or twice . . . or a zillion times," he says, rolling his eyes.

"Well, this PROVES it!" I say, handing him the fortune.

Francis reads it. He's making his constipated "I'm not so sure about this" face.

"Surpass all others?" he says. "Surpass them in WHAT?"

"I'm a man of many talents," I tell him. "It could be anything!"

Francis hands me back the fortune. "Not ANY-thing," he says with a smirk. "We can eliminate academic achievement as a possibility."

You're a riot, Francis. Just for that, I might not include you in my posse when I get rich and famous.

It'll be great to be rich. Then I can pay people to make my life easier. A chauffeur to drive me around. A brainiac to do all my homework. Somebody to buy all my clothes, so I don't have to go to the mall and try on pants in one of those cheesy little changing rooms. I hate that.

And I'll get a chef—somebody to cook me all kinds of good stuff. I'm STARVING right now. All I've got in my stomach is a couple of spoonfuls of lumpy oatmeal.

Hm. I guess I could eat this fortune cookie.

Oh, how I hate her.

"Is this true, Nate?" Mrs. Godfrey's voice cuts right through me as she heaves herself up from her chair.

Uh-oh. If Mrs. Godfrey catches you eating in class, it's an automatic detention. Pretty bogus, considering she keeps a stash of peanut butter cups in her desk. (Don't ask me how I know that. I have my ways.)

Yikes. She's moving fast!
Come on! CHEW!

Swallow! NOW!!

Phew. Just in
time. I choke
down the last
few crumbs half
a second before
she steams up
to my desk.

"Hmmm," she says, looking long and hard. "I don't

see anything. You must have been mistaken, Gina."

HA!! Gina's speechless! Her little plan to land me in trouble didn't work! How sweet is THAT?

Oh, boy. Announcements. The excitement never stops around here.

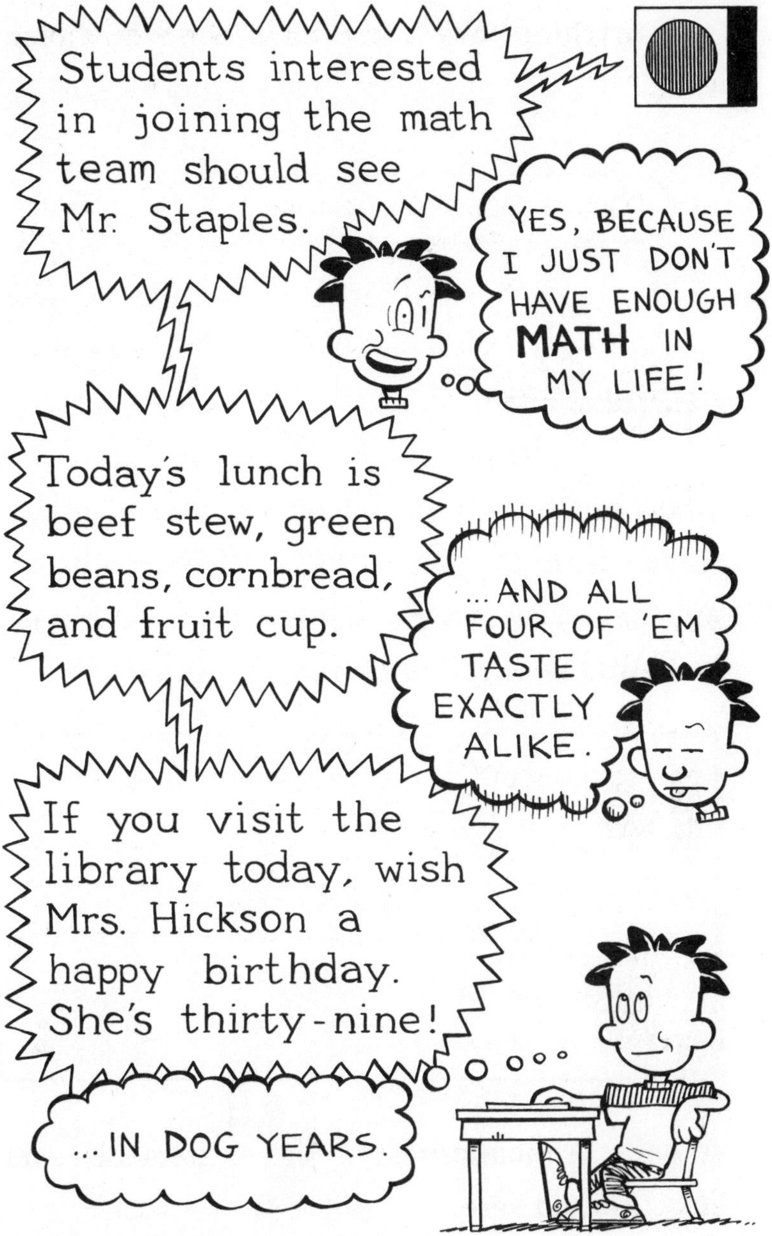
Students interested in joining the math team should see Mr. Staples.
YES, BECAUSE I JUST DON'T HAVE ENOUGH MATH IN MY LIFE!
Today's lunch is beef stew, green beans, cornbread, and fruit cup.
...AND ALL FOUR OF 'EM TASTE EXACTLY ALIKE.
If you visit the library today, wish Mrs. Hickson a happy birthday. She's thirty-nine!
...IN DOG YEARS.

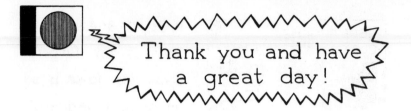

Thank you and have a great day!

That's it. Homeroom's over. So why am I still sitting here?

Because homeroom with Mrs. Godfrey is followed by first period social studies with . . . MRS. GODFREY! What a brutal way to start the day. Now I know where the phrase "rude awakening" comes from.

After social studies, there's nowhere to go but up. Here's the rest of my day:

PERIOD 2: ENGLISH
Ms. Clarke is okay, but shouldn't someone who teaches English actually make sense once in a while?

FOR A NONRESTRICTIVE CLAUSE OR PHRASE, BUT **NOT** FOR INDEPENDENT CLAUSES JOINED BY COORDINATING CONJUNCTIONS...

SAY WHAT?

PERIOD 3: ART

This is my favorite class. Mr. Rosa is so burned out, he doesn't even bother with lesson plans. Now that's teaching!

PERIOD 4: LUNCH

You eat as quick as you can. Then you spend the rest of the time checking out girls and throwing carrot sticks at Brad Macklin.

PERIOD 5: GYM

When you're playing floor hockey or dodgeball, it's awesome. When you're doing rhythmic gymnastics, you pray that nobody's around taking yearbook pictures.

PERIOD 6: MATH

Here's a multiple-choice question. Is math:

A) totally boring?

B) completely useless?

C) a great place to grab an afternoon nap?

D) all of the above?

The correct answer, of course, is D. Which was also my grade on the last test.

PERIOD 7: SCIENCE

The highlight of the year was when Mr. Galvin's dentures fell out during his lecture on earthquakes. That's when I gave him the nickname "Shifting Plates."

I give ALL the teachers nicknames. I know: EVERYbody invents funny names for teachers. But I WORK at it. That's why I'm the official nickname czar of P.S. 38.

A good nickname has a lot of stuff going on. One of my all-time best nicknames for Mrs. Godfrey is Venus de Silo. (I got the idea from a famous sculpture called "Venus de Milo.")

Venus was the goddess of love and beauty. Mrs. Godfrey isn't loving OR beautiful. So that makes it funny.

Venus is also the name of a planet. Mrs. Godfrey is a lot like a planet. She's huge, round, and gassy.

A silo is filled with feed for cows. Mrs. Godfrey reminds everyone of a cow, especially when she's eating.

And that's only ONE of her nicknames. I've got tons more. In fact, I can tell you exactly how many . . .

GODFREY NICKNAMES

1. Godzilla
2. Boring.com
3. Pass the Gravy
4. She Who Must Not Be Named
5. Dragon Breath
6. I Can't Believe She's Not Butter
7. Dark Side of the Moon
8. Extra Crispy
9. There's No Place Like Homework
10. Ozone
11. Queen Kong
12. Gas Station
13. Big Bang
14. Animal Planet
15. Wrecking Ball
16. Dullapalooza
17. El Guapo
18. Pardon My Nachos
19. Jaws
20. Venus de Silo

Twenty nicknames and counting! Not too shabby!

Yikes. Busted.

She looks at the list for a long time. Her face turns red, then white. I can see her jaw muscles working.

I wait for her to start shouting, but for the longest time she doesn't say a word. She just looks at me. That's worse than shouting.

Finally, she speaks.

She crumples up my list. Then she opens her desk drawer and pulls out a pad.

I've seen that pad before.

She writes something down, then hands me the slip. I notice a tiny smile at the corners of her mouth. But the rest of her looks mean.

"Take this to Mrs. Czerwicki at the end of the day," she tells me.

DETENTION REPORT

STUDENT: _Nate Wright_
TEACHER: _C. Godfrey_

REASON FOR DETENTION:

Insolence

"Insolence?" I say out loud. "What's that?"

"Here's a dictionary," Mrs. Godfrey snarls.

I bet it doesn't mean "destined for greatness."

CHAPTER 6

in·so·lence ('in(t)-s(ə-)lən(t)s), noun
1 : contemptuously rude or impertinent behavior or speech. **2 :** the quality or condition of being insolent.

"Turns out 'insolence' basically means acting like a brat," I say to Francis and Teddy as we walk to English.

I'm just about to give Teddy a notebook smackdown when I remember that he's going to share his lunch with me later. I decide to be nice to him.

SHUT UP, SCRUB.

I stuff Mrs. Godfrey's detention slip deep into my pocket. I'm not going to let one little detention ruin my whole day. Especially not after I got such an awesome fortune.

"What do you guys think 'You will surpass all others' means?" I ask.

"Probably that you got somebody else's fortune cookie by mistake." Teddy laughs.

"It doesn't just say 'You will surpass all others,'" Francis corrects me. "It says, 'TODAY you will surpass all others'!"

Hm. He's right. So the fortune will probably come true during school. At home, the only "others" for me to surpass are . . .

. . . Dad and Ellen. Big whoop.

"So if the fortune is real," I say, "I'm going to surpass all others sometime in the next . . ."

"I guess so." Francis shrugs. "You'd better work fast."

Ugh. Jenny and Artur. Excuse me while I gag.

Thanks, Francis. Feel free to stop talking anytime.

And, by the way, not EVERYBODY likes him. I'm not exactly president of the Artur Fan Club.

It's not like he's a major butthead or anything. I just hate that he's so GOOD at stuff—all the same stuff I'M good at. It's so obnoxious.

Things were a lot better before Artur came along.

ARTUR FACT:
He doesn't speak English all that great, which for some reason all the girls think is cute.

SEEING YOU LATERS!

SQUEAL!

HE'S ADORABLE!

Before Artur...	After Artur...
I was the #1 player on the chess team.	He knocked me down to #2.

Check-mate!

stunned expression

Nice tries, Nate!

Sigh...

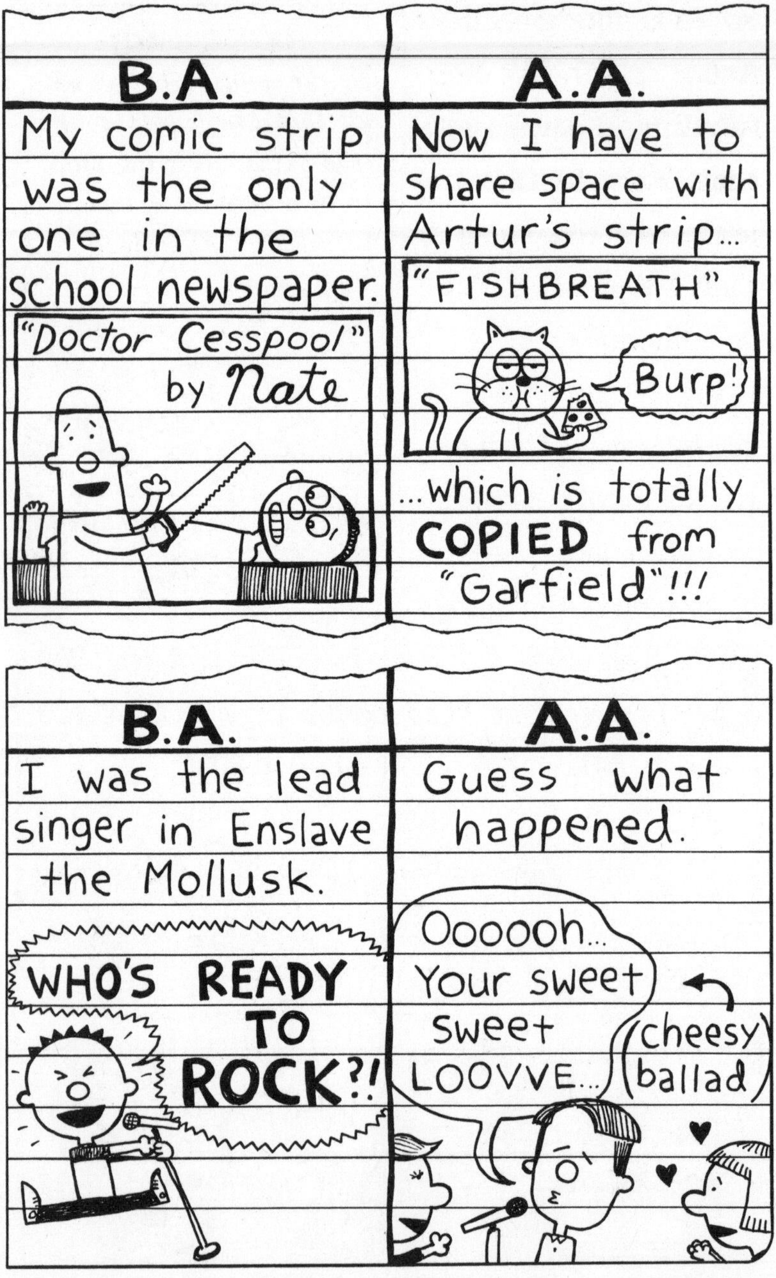

B.A.
My comic strip was the only one in the school newspaper.
"Doctor Cesspool" by Nate
A.A.
Now I have to share space with Artur's strip...
"FISHBREATH"
Burp!
...which is totally COPIED from "Garfield"!!!
B.A.
I was the lead singer in Enslave the Mollusk.
WHO'S READY TO ROCK?!
A.A.
Guess what happened.
Oooooh... Your sweet sweet LOOVVE...
(cheesy ballad)

So everybody thinks Artur is Mr. Wonderful. I can deal with that. But when he and Jenny started going out? That killed me.

I met Jenny in first grade. I've liked her ever since. And I'm positive that deep down she likes me, too, even though she ACTS like she hates me. I've always been 100 percent sure that someday the two of us are going to make an awesome couple.

Then Artur comes along. The next thing you know, they're acting like Romeo and Juliet all over the place. It's gross. It's sickening.

The FORTUNE!

"Today you will surpass all others!"

Could that have something to do with Jenny? Maybe the fortune means I'm going to surpass Artur! Maybe Jenny dumps HIM . . .

"Today we'll be finishing up our poetry unit," Ms. Clarke announces.

I used to think poetry was just a bunch of British dudes wearing tights and writing sonnets with a peacock feather, but there's a lot more to it. Ms. Clarke has taught us about all kinds of poetry. We have to write our own poems in a "poetry portfolio."

POETRY! PORTFOLIO!
Nate Wright

LIMERICK by Nate Wright

I have feasted on all sorts of noodles,
I have tried an assortment of strudels.
Of the foods that I've eaten,
Only one can't be beaten:
An extra large bag of Cheez Doodles.

Nate
great ←
date ←
fate ←
late ←
mate ←
rate ←
state

HAIKU by Nate Wright

You have Cheez Doodles.
Fresh. Crunchy. Puffalicious.
Give me one right now.

Duh.

what rhymes with "Duh"?

ODE TO A CHEEZ DOODLE by Nate Wright

I search the grocery store in haste,
To find that sweet lip-smacking taste.
And there it is, in aisle nine.
It's just a dollar thirty-nine!
A bag of Doodles most delicious.
Check the label: They're nutritious!
And do you know how satisfied
I feel while munching Doodles fried?
I savor each bright orange curl,
Until it seems I just might hurl.
Their praises I will always sing.
Cheez Doodles are my everything.

Yee-HA!

QUACK

Doodle
oodle
noodle
strudel
poodle
caboodle

ON OFF

ZAP

Ms. Clarke is still yakking away. "You may write any kind of poem you like," she says, "a funny poem, a serious poem, a love poem . . ."

JUNK food? Excuse me, but Cheez Doodles are NOT junk food. They're . . . YUMMY!

Hold it. Did Ms. Clarke say "love poem"?

A love poem! That just might work! Jenny goes wild for that sort of thing. She was all excited about a valentine Artur gave her last year, and that was only a lame store-bought card.

I look across the room at Jenny. She's busy picking lint balls off her sweater, but there's electricity between us. I can feel it.

A plan is forming in my brain.

STEP 1: I write a love poem to Jenny—but not a sappy, mushy one. One that says, "Why hang out with Artur when I'M available?"

STEP 2: I slip the poem into Jenny's notebook, when Artur's not stuck to her like Joe Velcro.

STEP 3: I sit back and wait for Jenny to fall madly in love with me.

I've never written a love poem before. But how tough can it be? All I've got to do is find a few words that rhyme with "Jenny."

GINA!!!! Why can't she mind her own stinkin' business?

I can feel my face turning beet red. I sneak a quick peek at the other side of the room.

Jenny's looking at me funny. So is Artur. Great.

Leave it to Gina to ruin everything. Now my plan has exactly zero chance of working.

GOOD-BYE, LOVE POEM!

RIP!! RIP!
RIP! RIP!
RIP! RIP!!

NATE?

And now here's Ms. Clarke. This just keeps getting better.

"Are you having trouble thinking of something to write about besides Cheez Doodles?" She smiles.

"Uh . . . yeah, sort of," I stammer.

"Poetry comes from the heart, Nate," she tells me. "That's where you'll find something to inspire you."

Uh, okay. I have no idea what she means, but I nod my head anyway. The whole class is staring at me.

I'm like, can we just move on?

Then I hear it. Nobody else does, but I do.

Gina laughs.

I shoot her a look. She's leaning back in her chair. She's got a nasty little smile on her face. Here I am looking like a fool in front of everyone— in front of JENNY—and Gina's loving every minute. SHE made this happen. This is her fault. The blood is pounding in my head. Ms. Clarke is saying something. I can barely hear her.

What does my heart tell me?

It tells me . . .

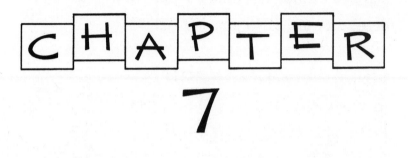

CHAPTER 7

"So let me get this straight," Francis says as we file out of the English classroom.

GINA'S THE ONE WHO SHOULD KEEP HER BIG FAT MOUTH SHUT?

HEH HEH!

"Well, she SHOULD," I grumble, waving the pink slip Ms. Clarke just handed me. "How come I get detention and GINA gets NOTHING?"

"Gina never gets in trouble," says Francis matter-of-factly. "She gets OTHER people in trouble."

Teddy takes the detention slip and reads out loud: "'Reason for detention: being disruptive in class, insulting a classmate.'"

Francis nods. "You WERE pretty insulting."

"Are you kidding?" I say. "That was NOTHING!
I can be WAY more insulting than THAT!"

It's about to turn into a no-holds-barred yo mama
throwdown when Francis interrupts us.

"Dudes!" he says, pointing excitedly. "Check it out!"

I look down the hall. Check WHAT out? Luke Bertrand and Amy Wexler are in a major lip-lock . . .

Matt Grover is giving Peter Hinkel a turbo-wedgie . . .

. . . and that weird girl whose name I can never remember is writing all over her arms again.

In other words, everything looks normal.

"What are we supposed to look at?" I ask Francis.

"Duh! The DISPLAY CASE!" he says.

P.S. 38 has two display cases. The one outside Principal Nichols's office is filled with all sorts of dusty trophies, boring spelling bee ribbons, and ancient pictures of the basketball team. (What's up with the UNIFORMS? It looks like they're wearing UNDERWEAR!)

P.S. 38 vs. DURHAM 1950

But the OTHER display case is cool. It's where Mr. Rosa puts all the best student artwork. He always chooses one student to feature on the center panel. There's a banner along the top that says:

If you've got the spotlight, it's like Mr. Rosa's telling everyone . . .

Hey! That could be it!!

If something by ME is in the spotlight, that means the fortune was RIGHT! I'll surpass all others!

I rush up to the display case. I bet my penguin sculpture is there.

Yeah, LAME drawings. Time for some feedback from Nate Wright, Art Critic.

Nice try, Ken, but you should probably stick to wood shop.

Sorry to burst your bubble, Amanda, but this looks like a bunch of sausages with legs.

I'm not sure about THAT hand, Tammy, but your OTHER hand can't draw very well.

"AGAIN?" I blurt out. "This is the second month in a row he's been on the center panel!"

"OLD SHOE" BY ARTUR

"Well, you have to admit," Teddy says, pressing up against the glass, "it's a pretty awesome drawing!"

"It's okay," I sniff.

"Okay?" Francis protests. "He's like a junior Picasso!"

Oh, yeah? Since when did Picasso make a career out of drawing SHOES?

Yeah, yeah. Everybody loves Artur.

This is so unfair. Why should HE be such an art star? I've done TONS of drawings that are better than that stupid SHOE of his. . . . Like THIS one!

LOOK at that! My drawing has it all: Action. Suspense. Potential bloodshed. This deserves to be in the spotlight just as much as ARTUR's drawing! Time to file an official protest.

Wha—? Frivolous requests?? FRIVOLOUS REQUESTS??

Puppet heads? I'm supposed to concentrate on puppet heads NOW?? This is an OUTRAGE!

I glance up at the door. The display case is only a few feet away. If Mr. Rosa won't put my drawing in that stinkin' case, I will.

Francis has his nose buried in the puppet head instructions:

He shoots me a suspicious glance. "Why are you whispering?"

"Ssh! No questions!" I hiss at him.

"ANY kind of diversion!" I say. "Just distract Mr. Rosa for five or ten seconds. That's all the time I'll need."

"Need for . . . ?" he starts to ask, but I shush him. Mr. Rosa is wandering over.

I give Francis a look that means: If you're REALLY my best friend, you'll do this for me.

He gives ME a look that means: You're a moron, but, hey, it's your funeral.

Good ol' Francis.

I ease over to the door. I wait for Francis to do his part.

PERFECT! The whole class cracks up, and while Mr. Rosa is trying to calm everybody down . . .

I sneak out . . .

. . . and PRESTO! I'm standing in front of the display case! That was almost too easy!

Now I just have to pop open this door . . . and I'll stick MY drawing right on top of Artur's! HA!

You've gotta be KIDDING me! It's STUCK! I yank and yank, but nothing happens . . .

. . . UNTIL THE KNOB BREAKS OFF!!

Holy cow, that was loud! Hope nobody . . .

Guess what Mr. Rosa pulls out of his back pocket?

Yup. A little pink pad.

I look at the slip he gives me. Where it says "Reason for Detention," he didn't even write anything.

He just drew a frowny face.

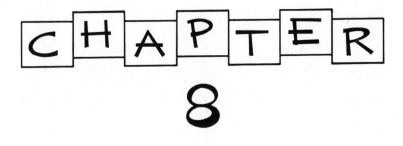

CHAPTER 8

It smells like egg salad, there aren't enough tables, and the walls are the color of cat puke. But after the morning I just had, I've never been so happy to walk into the cafeteria.

CAFETORIUM

Sorry. "Cafetorium." What a stupid word.

"I can't believe Mr. Rosa gave you a detention!"
Teddy says. "That's the first one he's handed out
all YEAR!"

"Chester took
our table," Teddy
says, and he's
right. Chester's
sitting where
I always sit,
looking like
the picture of
Java man in our
science textbook.

"Well," I snicker, "let's just ask him nicely to move."

Right. We all know you don't ask Chester for favors. Not unless you want to lose a few teeth. The kid once beat up his anger management counselor.

Finding somewhere else to sit could be sort of a challenge. Let's check out a few of our options:

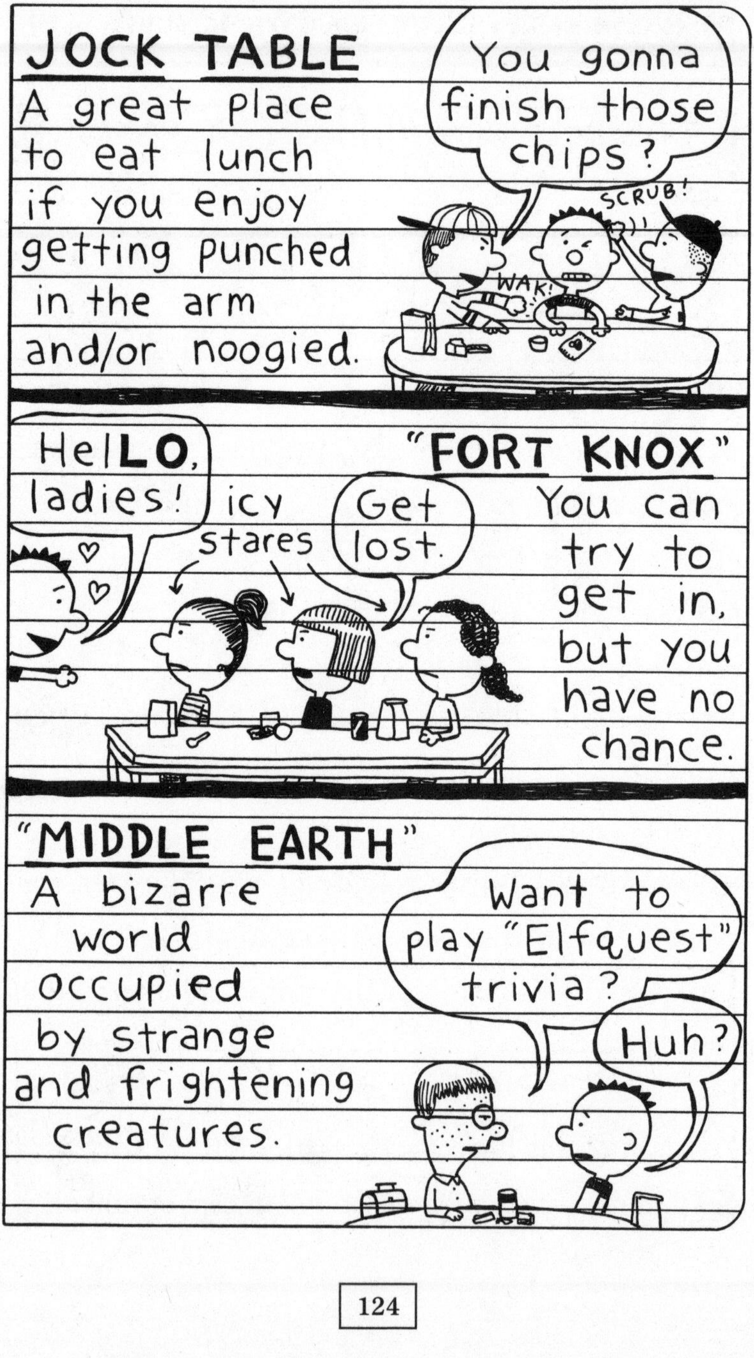
JOCK TABLE
A great place to eat lunch if you enjoy getting punched in the arm and/or noogied.
You gonna finish those chips?
SCRUB!
WAK!
HelLO, ladies!
icy stares
Get lost.
"FORT KNOX"
You can try to get in, but you have no chance.
"MIDDLE EARTH"
A bizarre world occupied by strange and frightening creatures.
Want to play "Elfquest" trivia?
Huh?

We decide to sit with our good friend Todd.

Whoops. Sorry, dude. (Mental note: Chubby kid with red hair and freckles is Chad, not Todd.)

"What are you reading?" Francis asks.

"*The Complete Book of World Records*," Chad says.

My ears perk up. World records? Hmm!

"What do you mean, ANOTHER one?" Francis jokes.

I ignore him and pull the fortune out of my pocket.

"This doesn't say, 'You will surpass your class-mates at P.S. 38,'" I declare. "It says, 'You will surpass ALL OTHERS'!"

I start flipping through Chad's book. There's got to be some record I could break. I just need to find the right one.

"Longest fingernails?"

Nope.

"Most tattoos?"
Don't think so.

"Is there a record for goofiest hair?" asks Teddy.

"Shut up," I say.

"Speed eating?" says Francis, looking skeptical.

"LOOK! Here's a guy who ate sixty hot dogs in ten minutes! And THIS guy ate forty-five slices of pizza in ten minutes!"

Thank you, Captain Obvious.

So what can I use to set a speed-eating record? We're racking our brains when we notice some kids about to dump their trays.

I can't hear what Francis is saying, but a few seconds later he's back at our table with . . .

Green beans?

"We have PLENTY of green beans!" Francis says.

"Riiiiiight!" says Teddy, catching on . . . "Because nobody EVER eats their green beans!"

Suddenly Francis and Teddy are zooming all over the lunchroom, asking everybody:

Before I know it, a pile of green beans the size of Mt. Everest is sitting on the table.

"Wait, these are NASTY," I say. "They look slimy."

"Perfect!" says Francis. "They'll slide right down!"

"I'm not hungry right now," I protest weakly. "Let's do this tomorrow."

This world record thing is beginning to seem a lot less cool. How did I get myself into this mess?

A crowd is beginning to gather. Francis sets his stopwatch. I guess there's no turning back now.

Ready . . .

    Set . . .

I grab a fistful of beans and jam them into my mouth. Cold bean juice dribbles down my chin as I chew once, twice, then swallow. They taste disgusting, but they do kind of slide right down. I shovel in another mouthful.

. . . then another . . . and another.

ONE
MINUTE
DOWN!

NINE
TO
GO!

One minute??? I've only been eating for one minute?

Oohhhhhhhhhh . . . I don't feel so good.

EAT!...EAT!...EAT!

The crowd is urging me on, but it's not working. My throat's all gaggy. I feel a little dizzy. Pieces of half-chewed beans are flying everywhere. Forget the world record; I'm hoping I don't throw up in front of half the school.

Uh-oh. I know that voice. Red alert.

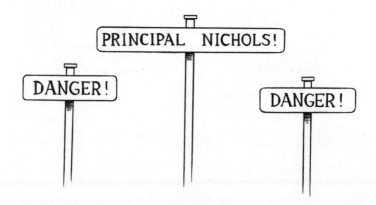

He was all nice and friendly when I ran into him earlier today. But he's not looking friendly now. My stomach does a triple somersault.

I start to talk, but this wad of beans in my mouth is cramping my style. I try to swallow it down, but I almost choke. It's just too big.

There's only one thing to do. I lean over the table and, trying to be as casual as I can . . .

. . . I spit out the beans.

Okay, relax, people. It's not all THAT gross. A pile of chewed-up green beans looks about the same as a pile of UNchewed-up green beans.

Principal Nichols looks a little green himself.

"I'm just . . . er . . . having lunch," I say.

"Lunch?" he repeats. "With the entire sixth grade cheering you on??"

"Well, I'm declaring lunch officially over," Principal Nichols growls. He looks at the green beans scattered all over the table and floor.

He starts for the door, and in that half second I see exactly what's about to happen. It seems

like it's in slow motion, but I can't do anything
to stop it.

Principal Nichols's foot lands in a puddle of slimy
bean juice,

AND . . .

For a minute, I can't tell if he's dead or alive.

Lucky me. He's alive.

And now I REALLY don't feel so good.

CHAPTER 9

MY BUTT'S ASLEEP.

Would it kill them to put a softer chair in here? This is like sitting on a toilet lid.

I try to ignore the pins and needles creeping down my legs. If Principal Nichols doesn't stop yakking soon, everything below my belly button will go numb.

He's lecturing me about the green beans. Yawn. I've heard this speech a zillion times. The words change a little bit, but it basically goes like this:

①. `DRAMATIC` RE-CREATION

Whatever it was that got me in trouble, Principal Nichols describes it *IN DETAIL*.

...Then you started eating the beans, making a **HUGE** mess! **THEN** you spit out a mouthful of beans on the table! And **THEN**...

Uh, yeah, I remember what happened. I was there.

②. *TWISTED SISTER*

He compares me to Ellen.

Your **SISTER** would *NEVER* engage in such behavior!

Nice. How would he like it if I compared him to other principals? (Not that I know any, but there **MUST** be some better ones out there.)

③ He uses the "P" word.

You have so much... **POTENTIAL!**

And this is news? Dude, I **KNOW** I have potential. I'm just **SAVING** it for something more important than school.

TAKE THIS SLIP TO MRS. CZERWICKI AT THE END OF THE DAY.

REASON FOR DETENTION: GREEN BEAN INCIDENT.

"Green bean incident"? That makes it sound like some sort of SCANDAL. Uh, HELLO? Earth to Nichols: I was trying to set a WORLD RECORD!

Not only that, his lecture dragged on past the fifth-period bell. Now I'm late for gym. Hey! Gym! THAT could be where I'll surpass all others!

Maybe I'm supposed to dominate in rope climbing or volleyball . . . or whatever Coach Calhoun has us doing today.

Except Coach Calhoun isn't here!

Coach John was P.S. 38's gym teacher back in the day. He retired, but the school keeps bringing him back as a sub. That might be fine for the school, but for us kids it's a complete nightmare. Because Coach John is insane.

COACH JOHN FACT: He enjoys showing everyone the scars from all his knee surgeries.

...AND THE **BONE** WAS POKING THROUGH THE **SKIN**!!

RUN, MAGGOTS, **RUN!**

Have you ever seen one of those war movies where the drill sergeant is a total psycho who's always screaming at everybody? Take away the uniform, and you've got Coach John.

I scoot around the bleachers, hoping to get into the locker room before he notices me. Not a chance. The man can't see his own feet, but somehow he spots ME right away.

Coach John's not real good with names.

See how warm and friendly he is?

I zip into the locker room. It's empty; that's a relief. Now I don't have to deal with Alan Ashworth and his Towel of Doom.

I jump into my shorts and T-shirt and head back to the gym when I spot myself in the mirror. I've still got dried green bean crud on my face. Nasty.

I'll just give it a quick rinse. I lean over the sink. . . .

RUB
SLOSH
SCRUB

WHAT THE...?

GAH!

Oh, NO!!! There was water on the countertop! It soaked right into my shorts!!!

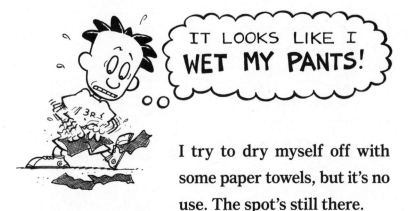

I try to dry myself off with some paper towels, but it's no use. The spot's still there.

This is a DISASTER!! What am I gonna do?? I can't walk around like THIS! It's like carrying a huge sign that says:

I look around frantically for another pair of

shorts. Nothing in the lockers. Nothing in the lost and found. Suddenly I remember that JENNY'S in my gym class. She'll think I'm a total idiot!

"What are you doing, changing into a TUXEDO?" Coach John bellows. "GET OUT HERE!!"

$=\ldots$ **NOW**!! $=$

Gulp. Looks like I have no choice . . . **BUT WAIT!!!**

There's a duffel bag tucked under a bench near the coaches' room. And sticking out of it is . . .

YES! What LUCK! I peel off my wet shorts and grab the dry ones. I don't care whose they are, I don't care what color they are, I don't care what size they are . . .

Okay, maybe I DO care about the size thing.

Holy cow, these are like CLOWN clothes! They're not even CLOSE to fitting!

1...

2...

3...

Yikes. Coach John's getting ready to snap, big time. I've gotta find a way to make these shorts stay on, and fast.

4...

Aha! There's a pile of towels by the showers. I grab a handful . . .

5...

6...

7...

8...

9...

. . . and start stuffing them down the shorts!

I know I look like a Dorkosaurus. But I found a way to keep these shorts up. And they don't have a giant wet spot on them.

WADDLE
WADDLE
WADDLE
WADDLE

I hustle into the gym. The whole class is lined up in rows, stretching out.

I hear a chuckle. Then another one. In five seconds, everybody's laughing like crazy.

Everybody but Coach John.

A joke? I have no idea what he means, but he looks like he's about to rip my arm off. I shake my head, afraid to say the wrong thing.

He slowly raises his hand and points at my shorts. I look at him, still baffled.

Then I see it.

A white "CJ" on Coach John's sweatpants.

I'm starting to get a very bad feeling. I look down at my shorts, and there it is: The same white "CJ."

Suddenly it hits me. Coach John thinks I'm making fun of him. That I'm showing off like I'm some sort of Coach John Mini-Me.

I can tell he's not hearing me. I can hardly hear mySELF. And all I can see is Coach John's giant face, turning about eight different shades of purple.

"We'll see if you're still laughing . . . ," says Coach John,

...AFTER YOU'VE RUN SOME GASSERS!

Perfect. Just how I wanted to spend fifth period:

running wind sprints.

In Coach John's shorts.

With a stomach full of green beans.

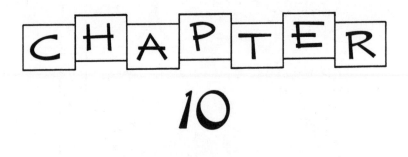

CHAPTER 10

Another pink slip. This is getting ridiculous.

"Coach John wrote me up!" I say angrily.

"'No respect for teacher,'" I read aloud.

That's messed up. What about HIM having no respect for ME? He didn't even bother to write my NAME!

"What's so funny?"
I snap.

"He's right!" Francis
says. "You DO have weird hair!"

Great. Now, on top of everything else, my so-called best friends are treating my head like a giant Slinky.

This day is really starting to bum me out. "Any more of this," I grumble, "and today just might make my list of Worst Days Ever."

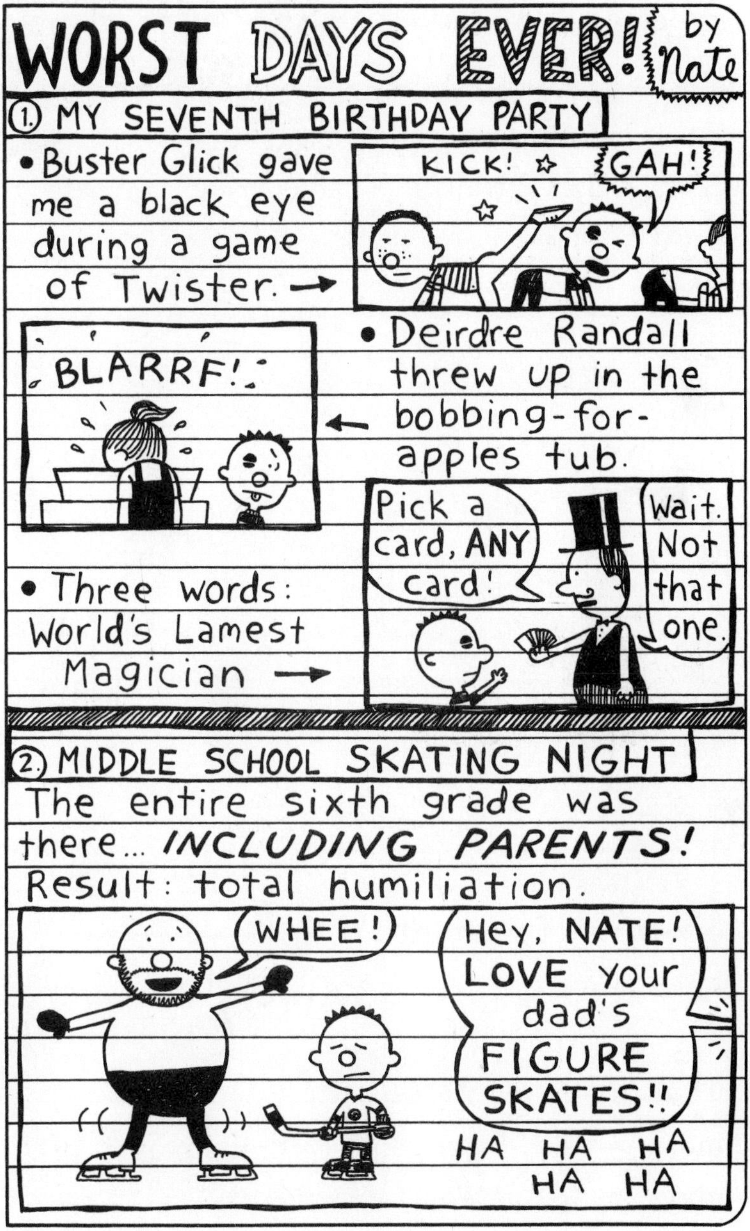
WORST DAYS EVER!
by Nate
1. MY SEVENTH BIRTHDAY PARTY
• Buster Glick gave me a black eye during a game of Twister.
KICK!
GAH!
BLARRF!
• Deirdre Randall threw up in the bobbing-for-apples tub.
• Three words: World's Lamest Magician
Pick a card, ANY card!
Wait. Not that one.
2. MIDDLE SCHOOL SKATING NIGHT
The entire sixth grade was there... INCLUDING PARENTS!
Result: total humiliation.
WHEE!
Hey, NATE! LOVE your dad's FIGURE SKATES!!
HA HA HA
HA HA

WORST DAYS EVER! (cont'd.)

③ "SPRING FEVER" DANCE

- That was the night Jenny and Artur officially started going out. (Meanwhile, I got stuck slow dancing with Kim Cressly.)

(Sigh!) Oh, Artur!

Stop stepping on my feet.

GURK!

④ SIXTH GRADE NATURE HIKE

HEY, KID! GET OUT OF THE POISON OAK!!

- I got yelled at by some crazy park ranger.

- I found out too late that the lock on the porta-potty was broken. →

YAHH!

Oop! Excuse me, Nate!

"Hold it," Francis points out. "You can't have a whole bunch of Worst Days Ever. By definition, there can only be ONE worst anything!"

Anyway, all I said was that today COULD make the list. It's not official yet. There's still a chance that this could turn into a GREAT day . . .

"I think you're trying too hard," Teddy declares.

"Whaddaya mean?" I ask.

"The whole FORTUNE thing! You're FORCING it! Just let it happen! ReLAX! Go with the flow!" Teddy says.

IN...
OUT...

IN...
OUT...

Go with the flow? What is this, a yoga retreat? I'm not going to surpass all others by sitting around doing deep breathing exercises.

"Let's move it, guys," says Francis. "We've got math."

Ugh. I hate math. I understand it fine, but my brain shuts down when Mr. Staples says stuff like:

The rest of my life. I can't wait.

We head into the math room. Right away, I can tell something's wrong.

Mr. Staples isn't watering his plants or writing problems on the board. He's not chatting with students or telling them horrible knock-knock jokes.

"What's wrong with Mr. Staples?" I whisper. "He's just SITTING there."

"Well, what's he SUPPOSED to be doing?" Teddy asks.

"Dancing on the desk?"

Teddy doesn't get it. But I do. I know trouble when I see it.

"Take your seats, everyone," Mr. Staples says.

The classroom gets quiet. That's weird. Mr. Staples NEVER tells us to take our seats. Suddenly everyone else is noticing what I've already realized: Something bad is about to happen.

"Please put away your books and binders," he instructs us.

"You have thirty minutes," Mr. Staples says, passing out the quizzes. "Please read the instructions carefublah blah blah blah blah blah blah blah blah blah blah blah. . . ."

While he babbles away, I quickly scan the quiz sheet.

Solve for the unknown value:
1. x ÷ 43 = 1,150
2. y ÷ 50 = 92
3. n ÷ 14 = 714
4. t ÷ 60 = 49

Find the mean, median, and mode:
5. 31, 169, 3, 38, 165, 105, 169, 64
6. 168, 44, 62, 25, 189, 26, 129, 92, 148, 62

Write each as a fraction:
7. 0.16
8. 0.36
9. 0.625

10. Twenty-one less than 4 times a number is 31. What is the number?

11. 2,000 and 11,000,000 added to a number is 11,110,184. What is the number?

12. What is 5/9 of 6579?

Only twelve questions? Hey, that's not too bad! I should be able to handle twelve questions in thirty minutes.

Away I go. Look, I already told you I'm not crazy about math. But you don't have to LIKE something to be good at it. I work my way down the page.

This one's easy . . .

. . . and so's that one.

. . . and that one and THAT one. Holy cow, I'm CRUSHING these questions! This is a BREEZE!

I finish the last problem, check my answers, and put down my pencil. Done!

And check THIS out! I finished TEN MINUTES EARLY!

I look around the room.

Teddy's still working . . .

Francis is still working . . .

EVERYONE'S still working!!

I'm the first one finished! My superior brain-power has blown everybody else away. Hey! I'VE SURPASSED ALL OTHERS!

Today will surpass others.

THE FORTUNE HAS COME TRUE!

Okay, I'll admit that surpassing all others on a math quiz isn't as exciting as setting a world record, but at this point I'll take anything.

I sneak a peek behind me. Even GINA'S still working! HA! I can't wait to see the look on her face when she realizes that I ACED this quiz and SHE . . .

Yeah, hear that, everyone? Pass 'em in!

Wait. Check your answers front . . . and . . . back? Did he say BACK??

I flip my quiz over. My eyes feel like they're about to pop out of my skull.

There ARE!
EIGHT more
questions!
Eight ques-
tions I DIDN'T
EVEN SEE!!!

Everyone else
is handing in
their quizzes.
In a total panic,
I grab my pen-
cil. I don't even
know what I'm writing. I just start scribbling
numbers at random.

"I'll take that, Nate."

I flinch.

Mr. Staples is stand-
ing at my desk. He
grabs my paper.

NO!! I can't pass it in with almost half the questions BLANK! I pull the page away from him.

"Time's UP, Nate," he growls, trying to take it from me. I hang on tight. All I need is a couple more minutes!

But Mr. Staples wants my quiz NOW. He pulls on the sheet hard. Suddenly I'm in a full-scale tug-of-war with my math teacher.

And I just lost.

"I'll trade you," Mr. Staples says through clenched teeth. He snatches the torn paper from my hand. "You give me THAT . . ."

A pink slip. All I was trying to do was finish the stinkin' math quiz. Instead, here I am with another detention.

Teachers always say they'll be happy if you just do your best. But when you TRY to do your best, they don't LET you.

Something about that just doesn't add up.

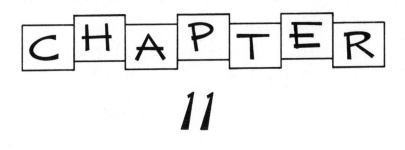

CHAPTER 11

"This stupid fortune," I complain, crumpling the paper into a tiny ball, "has been nothing but trouble."

"How would your face like to entertain my fist?"
I snap.

"Nate, the day's not over yet!" says Francis.

"Wake up, Rip Van Dorkle," I say. "Nothing good
ever happens in science."

"Professor Chuckles," Teddy snickers. "That's funny."

"Don't let Mr. Galvin hear you call him that," Francis says. "HE won't think it's funny."

"He never thinks ANYTHING'S funny!" I point out.

> HE'S STIFF AS A BOARD.

"You can say that again," says Francis.

Something just CLICKED!

"Guys, that's IT!" I say excitedly. "The way for me to surpass all others! I'll do something NOBODY'S ever done! I'll make Mr. Galvin LAUGH!"

Francis stares at me like he thinks I'm crazy.

"You're crazy," he says. "Don't you remember when we looked at all those old yearbooks in the library?"

Sure I do. We were trying to find funny pictures of teachers—bad haircuts, goofy-looking clothes, stuff like that. We dug out a bunch of yearbooks going back thirty or forty years. It was hilarious.

Mr. Galvin's been teaching at P.S. 38 since the Jurassic period. (Another one of my nicknames for him is G-Rex.) So we found plenty of pictures of him.

There were formal shots. (Has Mr. Galvin ever been INformal?)

There were candids. (You can't call them action shots since he's such a fossil.)

Mr. Galvin—Science

"Stand back, everyone. This bow tie is radioactive."

There was even a photo of him from his "hair replacement system" phase.

All the photos had one thing in common: Mr. Galvin wasn't smiling in any of them.

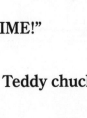

HA HA HA HA HA

NICE PLUGS!

"If nobody's ever seen him SMILE," Francis says as we head for the science lab, "how do you expect to make him LAUGH?"

"Hey, if anybody can do it, *I* can!" I say. "I crack people up ALL THE TIME!"

"Yeah, but not on purpose." Teddy chuckles.

RRRIIINNGGG!!

The bell. That's my cue. Let the laughs begin!

I decide to start with some good old-fashioned visual humor. There's nothing like a few strategically placed pencils.

"Nuts," I say as I reach my desk. "No reaction."

"Here's a reaction," Teddy says. "I'll never, EVER borrow a pencil from you again."

"I'm just warming up," I say. "Watch THIS! I'm going to PLAN B!"

"Please open your textbooks to page . . . ," Mr. Galvin starts to say. I raise my hand.

"Mr. Galvin? I have a science question for you," I say.

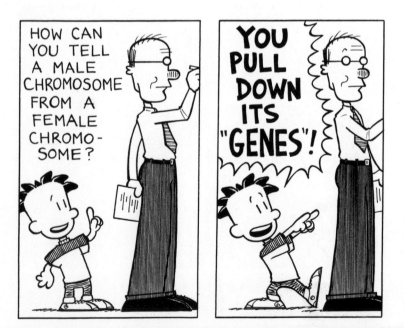

Wait, was that a hint of a smile? Did he start to laugh for just a half second?

Guess not.

"Psst! Mr. Comedy!" Francis whispers. "You're BOMBING!"

"Butt out," I hiss back. "I still haven't hit him with my best material!"

I pull a page from my notebook. It's a "Doctor Cesspool" comic I've been working on, and it's almost done. I whip out my drawing pen and put the finishing touches on the last panel.

"Mr. G.," I say, approaching his desk, "I have something to show you!"

He doesn't look up.

"Absolutely!" I answer. I hand him the comic. "The main character is a DOCTOR!"

The wacky adventures of...
DOCTOR
CESS-
POOL!!
Read on! →

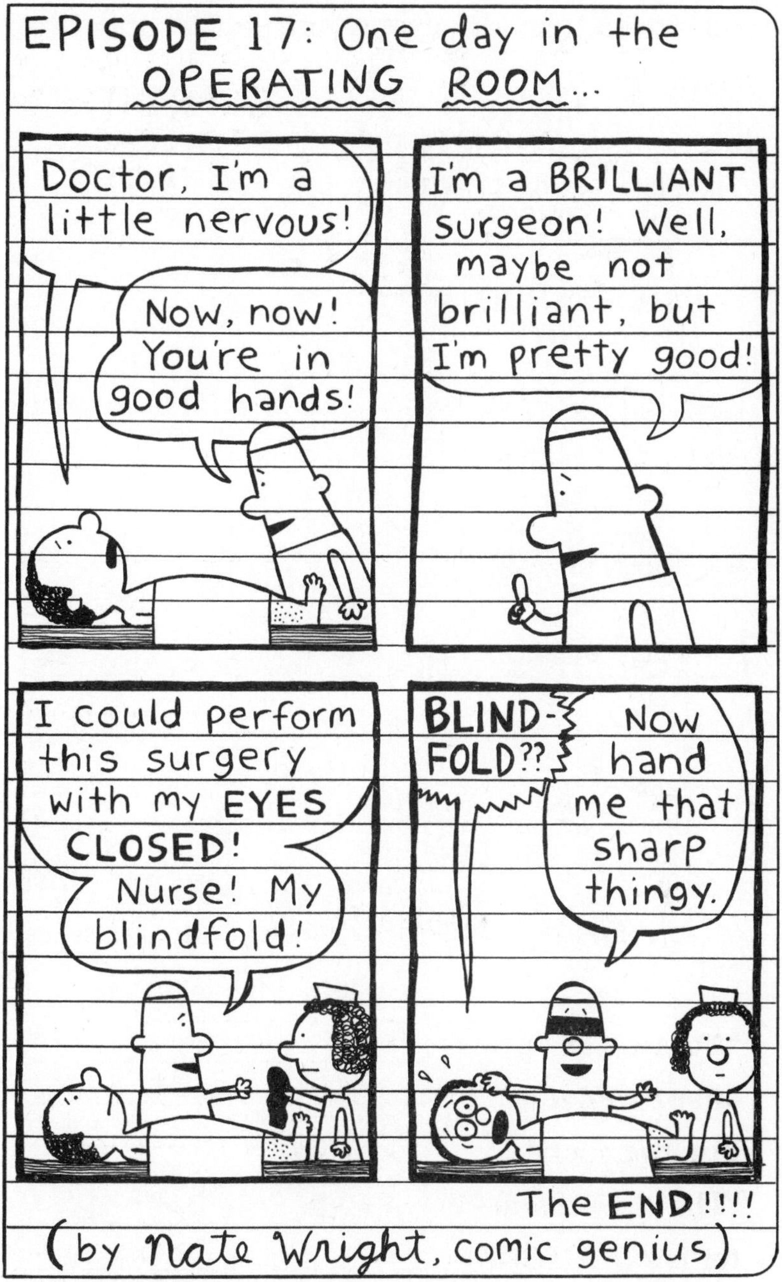
EPISODE 17: One day in the OPERATING ROOM...
Doctor, I'm a little nervous!
Now, now! You're in good hands!
I'm a BRILLIANT surgeon! Well, maybe not brilliant, but I'm pretty good!
I could perform this surgery with my EYES CLOSED!
Nurse! My blindfold!
BLIND-FOLD??
Now hand me that sharp thingy.
The END!!!!
(by Nate Wright, comic genius)

He doesn't laugh. Pretty much the opposite, actually.

"You're wasting my time, young man," he says.

He jams my pen— my special drawing pen!—into his shirt pocket. Rats. I'll never see THAT again.

I trudge back to my seat.

"You're striking out, champ," Teddy whispers.

"You're just not tickling his funny bone."

It's worth a try. It's not like anything ELSE is working.

There's a feather duster over by the supplies cabinet. Mr. Galvin uses it to keep the test tubes and beakers clean.

Easy now.
Gotta be casual
about this. I'll
just ease up
behind him

"I was . . . I was just . . . uh . . . ," I start.

"QUIET!" he roars. "Just go to your desk and STAY there! And if I hear another PEEP out of you . . ."

What choice do I have? I shuffle to my desk, flop down into my chair, and stare straight ahead . . .

. . . at a tiny little dot on Mr. Galvin's shirt.

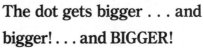

The dot gets bigger . . . and bigger! . . . and BIGGER!

My PEN! The cap must have come off inside his pocket!

And here's the funny part: He hasn't even NOTICED!

Yes, he has.

He stares me down. "Do you find this AMUSING, Nate?"

I know I should say no. Or at least try to keep a straight face. But something about that mondo ink stain on Mr. Galvin's shirt is just . . . well . . .

HILARIOUS!!

I try to hold it in. I really do. But I can't. By the time I pull myself together, Mr. Galvin is handing me a pink slip for five hours of detention.

Maybe someday I'll look back on this and laugh.

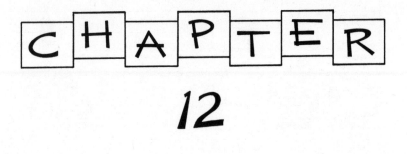

CHAPTER 12

It's 2:59.

School's over in exactly one minute. On a normal day, I'd be Mr. Happy right about now. I'd be counting down the seconds, ready to jump out of my seat, making plans about how to spend the rest of the afternoon:

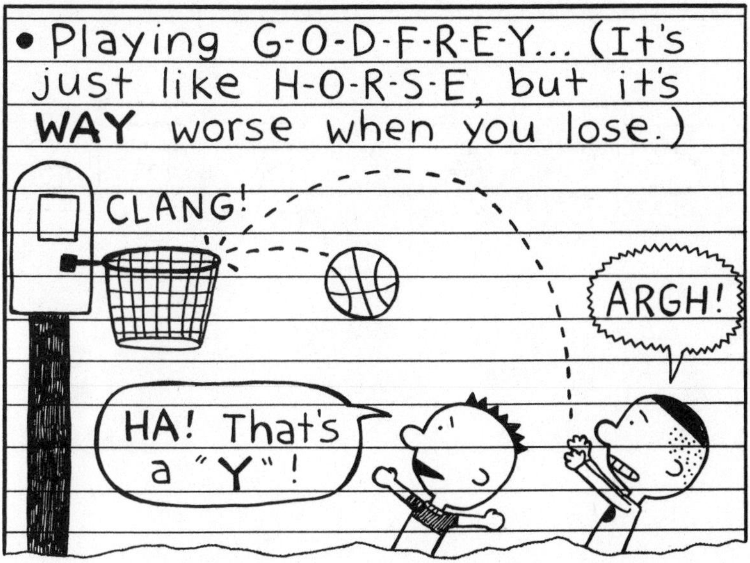
• Playing G-O-D-F-R-E-Y... (It's just like H-O-R-S-E, but it's **WAY** worse when you lose.)
CLANG!
ARGH!
HA! That's a "Y"!

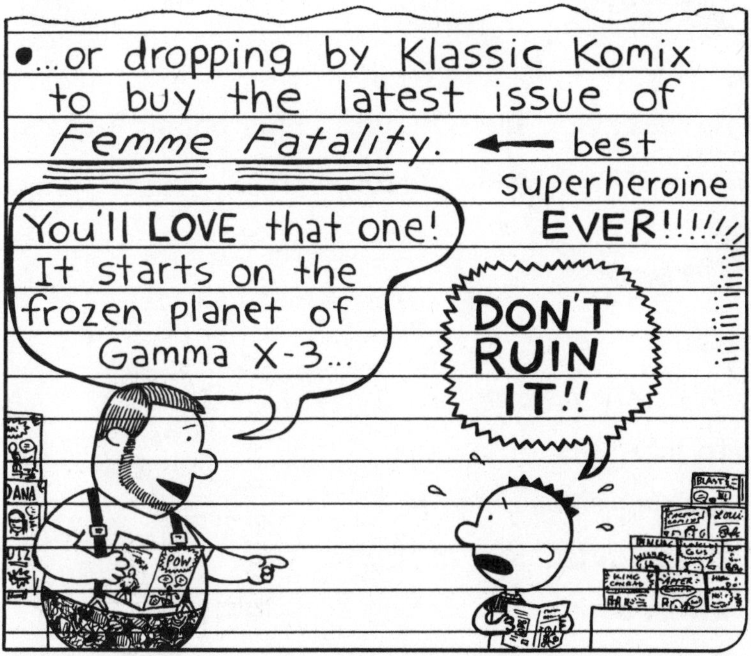
• ...or dropping by Klassic Komix to buy the latest issue of *Femme Fatality*. ← best superheroine **EVER**!!!!!!
You'll **LOVE** that one! It starts on the frozen planet of Gamma X-3...
DON'T RUIN IT!!

But there hasn't been anything normal about today since . . . since . . .

Hm. Guess the bell must have rung. Everybody's leaving.

As in leaving the building. Going home. And I'm not just talking about kids.

SO LONG, NATE! HAVE A NICE DAY!

"Have a nice day"? Is he serious? First of all, the day's over. Second, he already KNOWS I'm not having a nice day, since HE'S one of the people who STARTED this whole detention convention.

Teachers are such dopes sometimes. And by "sometimes," I mean "always."

The place empties out in no time. And before I know it . . .

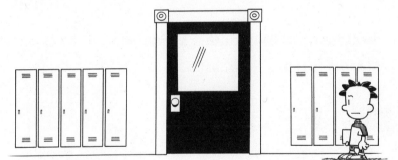

. . . it's just me.

There's nothing more sickening than being stuck in school when classes are over. Try it sometime.

It feels totally wrong. You can almost hear the walls talking trash.

Shut up, walls.

No sense putting it off. I head for the detention room.

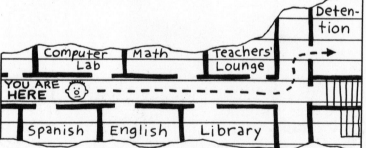

I admit I've had my share of detentions. I'm there so much, Teddy even made up a joke about it:

I didn't say it was a GOOD joke.

My last detention was the day
of the chess club bake sale.

Francis and I were running the table. We were
making some pretty good money, mostly from
selling Francis's mom's lemon squares, which
are awesome.

NOTE: NOBODY
WAS TOUCHING
DAD'S COCONUT
YOGURT PIE.

It was crowded. I noticed a kid named Randy Betancourt taking one of the lemon squares, real casual-like, and palming it in his hand.

He didn't pay. He just started walking away.

He acted all innocent. "Pay up for what?" he said.

He chucked the lemon square away, and . . .

. . . IT HIT MRS. GODFREY!

Nobody had noticed me and Randy arguing, but EVERYBODY stopped and looked when that lemon square smacked into Mrs. Godfrey's butt.

And of course she believed him. Shocker. Did she even ask for MY side of the story?

She pulled out her little pink pad and started writing me up. Randy stood beside her, giving me one of those "you got in trouble and I didn't" looks.

That's when I heard the voice inside my head:

GET YOUR MONEY'S WORTH

I was already getting detention, right? Might as well get punished for doing SOMETHING than for doing NOTHING.

So I did some-thing.

DAD'S COCONUT YOGURT PIE

I ended up with FIVE detentions that day. But I made sure Randy got what he deserved.

That's what bugs me about all the detentions I got today:

I walk in. Some days there are other kids, but today it's just me and Mrs. Czerwicki.

MRS. CZERWICKI FACT: *During detention, she passes the time by reading cheesy romance novels with titles like* Flames of Longing *and* Pounding Surf.

She puts down her book.

"AGAIN, Nate?" she asks with a sigh. I just shrug.

Did you hear that? "Slip." Singular. The old gal's pacemaker is about to get a major jolt.

"There's . . . uh . . . more than one, actually," I say, fishing in my pocket.

Mrs. Czerwicki raises an eyebrow. "How MANY more?" she says.

I lay a wad of pink papers on her desk. It looks like a mutant origami.

"Nate," she asks, "just how many teachers wrote you up?"

"All of 'em," I say . . .

Mrs. Czerwicki looks a little stunned. She spreads out the slips on her desk like she's playing solitaire.

She shakes her head. "Nate . . ."

"Record?" I repeat. "What kind of record?"

"Over the years, several students have received four detentions in a single day. A few have had five. One even got six."

Wait. "Does that mean I've . . ."

Mrs. Czerwicki grimaces. "Well . . . I suppose you could put it that way."

"It came true!" I shout.

"IT CAME TRUE!"

Mrs. Czerwicki looks totally confused, which is nothing new. She takes off her glasses, rubs her eyes, and says, "Please sit down, Nate."

Sit down? Gladly! I practically dance over to my desk.

On the desktop, there's a drawing I made the last time I was here. (You're not supposed to draw on the desks, but what do they EXPECT us to do during detention? Just SIT here?)

Hey, I never SIGNED this! I sneak a glance to make sure Mrs. Czerwicki's not looking. Then I pull out a pencil and write at the bottom:

by Nate Wright
SCHOOL RECORD HOLDER!

"School record holder."

NOW
THAT'S
GREATNESS!

Okay, so it's not going to get me one of those display case trophies. But, hey, a record's a record. I'm officially a part of P.S. 38 history. When you think about it, getting all those detentions turned out to be pretty lucky.

I can hardly believe my good fortune.

Lincoln Peirce

BIG NATE STRIKES AGAIN

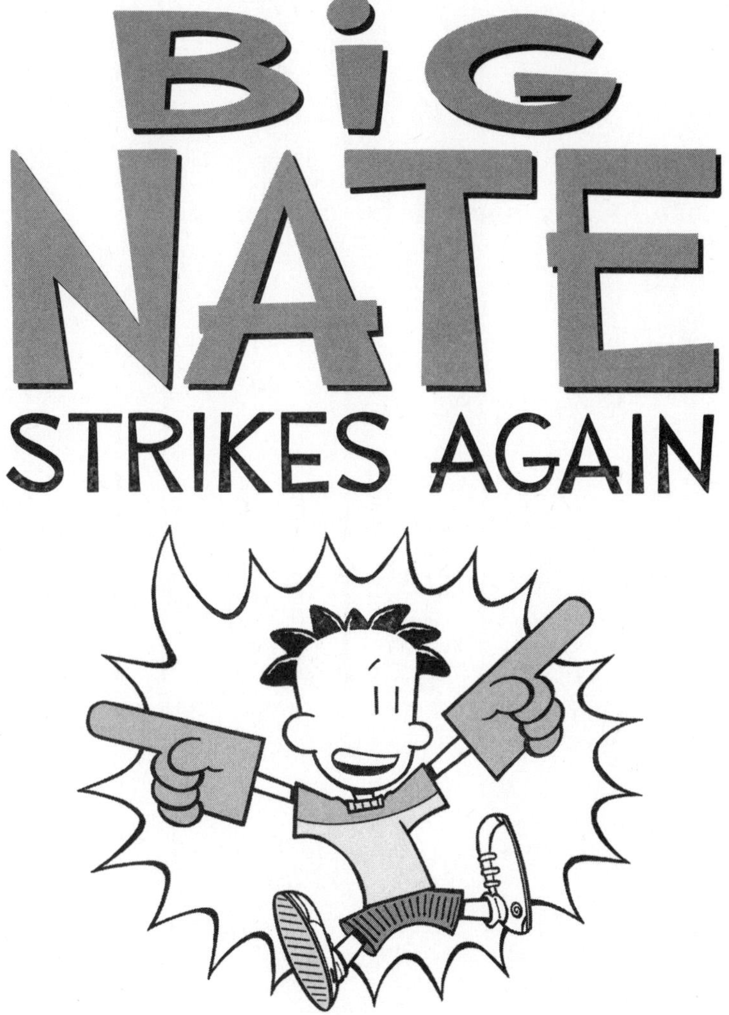

To Elias, from your friend and admirer

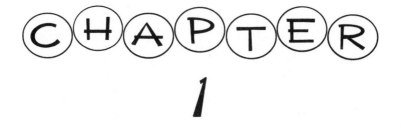

CHAPTER 1

"That's the ugliest baby I've ever seen."

Teddy and I are standing in the entrance hall of our school, P.S. 38, in front of a bulletin board covered with a gajillion baby pictures. I've never seen so much pink and blue in my life.

"Which one?" I chuckle, peering over his shoulder for a closer look.

What?? Hey, WAIT a minute! . . .

"It IS??" Teddy says. He's trying to act all shocked, but I can tell by the look on his face he knew it was my picture all along.

"Yup. That's Nate, all right," says Francis, walking up behind us.

Francis and Teddy are my two best friends—which might surprise you, considering how they're ragging on me about this baby picture. But that's just the way the three of us operate. They both know it's only a matter of time before I find something to bust THEIR chops about. It all evens out in the end.

"Well, what about YOU, Francis?" I say, quickly locating his photo on the board.

Francis shrugs. "Hey, ALL babies are kind of chunky," he says. "Where do you think the phrase 'baby fat' comes from?"

"From your picture, obviously," snorts Teddy.

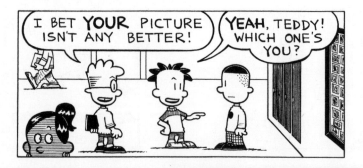

He waves at all the photos on the board.

Before Francis and I give Teddy a tag-team noogie for being so obnoxious, maybe I should explain what's up with all these baby pictures.

This is Mrs. Shipulski's bulletin board. She's the school secretary, and she's in charge of what goes on it. Usually it's covered with lame posters, like:

 or . . .

But last week Mrs. Shipulski decided to try something different. Here's what happened:

Actually, that last part didn't really happen. I just wanted to jazz up the story.

Anyway, that's how the P.S. 38 Guess That Baby game got started. Mrs. Shipulski asked every single kid in the sixth grade to put a picture on this board.

"Some of these are so easy to guess," Francis says.

"And there's Chester," Teddy says, pointing at another one.

I'm not really listening to Teddy and Francis. I'm scanning the board from left to right, searching for one . . . specific . . . picture.

There! Sandwiched between a couple of kids having really bad hair days—that's her!

AH-HA!

"Who'd you find?" Francis asks.

"Take a look!" I say.

Francis and Teddy step up to examine the picture more closely. They look confused. As usual.

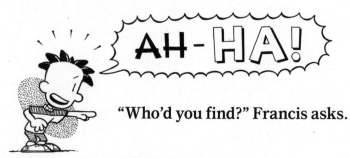

"I give up," Teddy says finally. "Who is it?"

"Isn't it OBVIOUS?" I say.

Jenny's the most awesome girl in the whole sixth grade, and someday she and I are going to make a great couple. (Unfortunately, she's going out with Artur at the moment, which is kind of a drag. But that'll change.) The point is, I'm a Jenny expert.

"I recognized her right away," I go on. "She's the best-looking baby here. By FAR!"

Ugh. Look who just oozed in. Gina. How is this any of HER business?

"Of COURSE I'm sure," I snap at Gina. "I'm POSITIVE!"

"Oh, really?" says Gina with an obnoxious little smirk. "Well, maybe you don't know her as well as you THINK you do!"

She marches over to the board . . .

. . . and starts pulling the picture off.

"Hey, you can't do that!" I shout. "That's not yours!"

Gina walks toward me. "Well, if it's not mine," she asks . . .

She holds it up close to my face. There, written on the back, I see:

Gina Hemphill-Toms   age 14 months

I blink hard and look again, hoping that maybe I read it wrong. But there's no mistake. This isn't a picture of Jenny. It's Gina. I feel like I just got clubbed on the forehead with a Louisville Slugger.

With a nasty grin, Gina throws my own words
back at me:

Teddy and Francis explode with laughter. So do
some other kids who've started to crowd around.
And there's nothing I can do about it. This is like
one of those bad dreams where everyone else has
clothes on and you're in your underwear.

Gina puts the picture back, then walks away, waving at everybody like a stinkin' prom queen.

I just might puke. Here I am, standing in front of half the school, looking like a visitor from Planet Moron. But I can deal with that. I've done it before. What makes this the absolute pits is knowing that it was Gina who got the best of me.

Gina's one of my least favorite people. No, more than that. She's one of my least favorite ANYTHINGS. Check out my list:

THINGS I CAN'T STAND!

by: 👤 ← Nate Wright, esq.

(notice: **NOT** listed in order!)

- ☹ Cats (ESPECIALLY when they haven't been declawed)
- ☹ Egg Salad
- ☹ Social Studies
- ☹ **School Picture Day** ➡
- ☹ Crusty, dried-up "erasers" that don't even work. They SMUDGE everything!
- ☹ Standardized tests
- ☹ Being sick during the weekend
- ☹ Math
- ☹ "Oldies" music
- ☹ **Figure skating** ➡
- ☹ Bubble gum that loses its flavor in twenty seconds
- ☹ Barbers who have no idea what "a little off the top" means.
- ☹ Squishy bananas
- ☹ Shopping
- ☹ **Gina** ⬛➡
- ☹ Paper cuts
- ☹ Parent-teacher conferences
- ☹ Any art project involving egg cartons or pipe cleaners

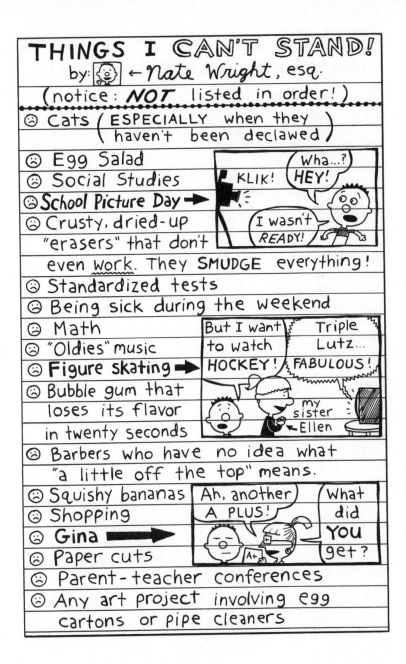

KLIK! Wha...? HEY! I wasn't READY!

But I want to watch HOCKEY! Triple Lutz... FABULOUS! my sister Ellen

Ah, another A PLUS! What did YOU get? A+

That makes it pretty clear, right? When you're comparing someone to egg salad and figure skating, that's about as low as it gets.

"Oh, come on," says Francis. "You don't HATE her."

"Yes, I do," I growl.

"Well, just remember what they say," Teddy says with a smile. "It's a fine line between hate and . . ."

Francis snickers. "You two will make a LOVELY couple," he says when he finally pulls himself together.

I'm about to knock their heads together, Three Stooges style . . .

. . . when the bell rings for homeroom.

I'm no fan of homeroom—hey, it's ten minutes of sharing oxygen with Mrs. Godfrey—but I'm all for anything that'll shut up Francis and Teddy. In I go.

New seat assignments? Fine. Whatever. I don't really care where I sit. I just want class to start so I can put all this Gina stuff . . .

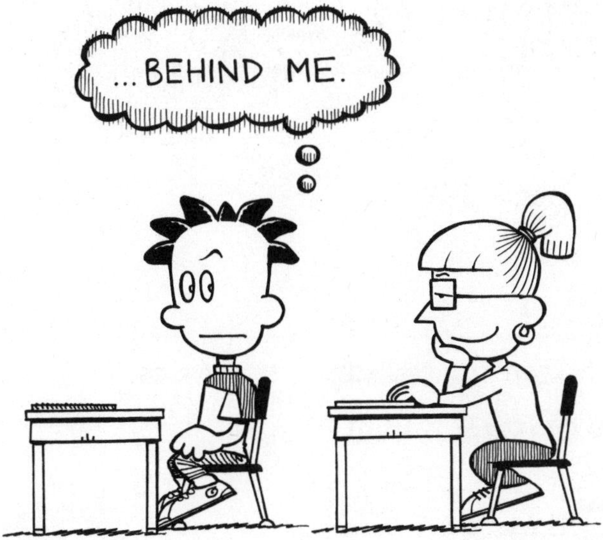
...BEHIND ME.

CHAPTER 2

You're probably wondering: What's up with Nate drinking all the Gina Hater-ade? Is she really that bad?

Uh, that would be a yes. With a capital Y.

It's tough to say what it is about Gina that bugs me the most. There's so much to choose from. But here's a big one: She's always talking about how GREAT she is.

Francis says that maybe Gina just ACTS like she's better than everybody else because deep down she doesn't really like herself. He might have a point. If I were Gina, I wouldn't like myself either. But Gina's taking up way too much space in my brain this morning. I really need to start thinking about something else.

Like the fact that class started five seconds ago, and Mrs. Godfrey's already yelling.

And now she's pulling out her blue folder. Oh, no.

Mrs. Godfrey color codes everything. Her yellow folder is for attendance sheets. The green one is for homework assignments. The red one's filled with in-class work sheets. And the blue one?

"Special projects." And I don't mean special in a good way. In middle school, "special" is like a dirty word.

The last time we did a special project, Mrs. Godfrey only gave me a C plus on my Louisiana report because she said I wrote too much stuff about pelicans. HELLO!? The pelican happens to be the state bird of Louisiana! That was vital info!

And the time before that, she gave me a lousy grade on my replica of the Colosseum because

I built it out of Legos. Well, what did she EXPECT me to do? Go to the nearest quarry and dig up some marble?

"I'm going to tell you about a new special project, class," Mrs. Godfrey announces. She's smiling, which is never a good sign. Plus, whenever she shows her teeth it reminds me of a shark attack on Animal Planet.

Ugh. A research paper. That's a biggie. Those things take weeks to do. And they usually count a ton toward your semester grade.

"AND . . . ," she continues . . .

YES!! Finally, some good news!

I look over at Teddy and Francis. I can tell we're all thinking the same thing. We jump up from our chairs and head straight for the front of the room.

She looks like she just smelled something foul. "I don't THINK so," she says.

SPECIAL PROJECT FACT:
The only time she let the three of us work together, we built a model of Mount Vesuvius and accidentally splattered her with fake lava.

WHOOPS.

"First of all, you will be working in PAIRS, not groups of three," she says, sounding like she expected us to know that already. "And SECOND of all . . . I'll be matching students RANDOMLY."

She pulls out a cookie jar from her bottom drawer. Not that there are any cookies in it, of course. She probably ate them all. She sure didn't offer US any.

"I'll select two names at a time," Mrs. Godfrey explains. "The classmate you're paired with will be your partner for this project."

Wow. This is like one of those lottery drawings on TV, where a babe picks numbered Ping-Pong balls out of a giant fish tank. Except Mrs. Godfrey's not using Ping-Pong balls. And she's not a babe.

The class starts buzzing. We all understand the stakes.

You could end up with someone great, or you could get stuck with a total dud.

The best partners are pretty obvious: Francis or Teddy would be fantastic. Getting paired with Jenny would be beyond awesome. And of course whoever gets paired up with ME is hitting a major jackpot.

But in every class, there are always a few kids like this:

The suspense is killing everybody. What's the holdup here? Mrs. Godfrey's just standing by her desk, staring at us.

Oh. I get it. She's doing that thing teachers always do, when they get all quiet and wait for the class to figure out that it's time to shut up.

Finally she reaches into the jar and picks out the first two slips. "Kendra . . . ," she reads aloud, ". . . and Matthew."

I shoot a quick look at Kendra and Matthew. They don't exactly look thrilled, but I'm pretty sure they both realize one thing:

Mrs. Godfrey continues . . .

"Brian and Kelly . . . Molly and Allison . . . Jenny and Artur . . . Kim and Nick . . . Cindy and Steven . . ."

Wait, hold it. Rewind. Did I hear that right?

Great. Those two are practically joined at the hip as it is. Now they'll be spending even MORE time together. This is an OUTRAGE!

Oh, come ON! First Jenny and Artur, and now Teddy and Francis get to work together? Look at them over there. They're acting like they just won a trip to Disney World.

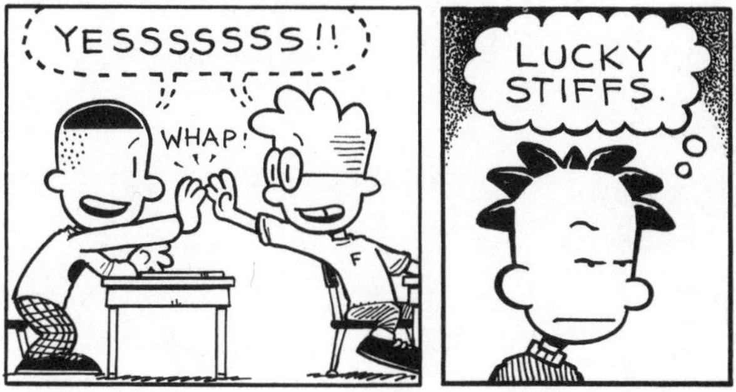
YESSSSSSS!!
WHAP!
LUCKY STIFFS.

But what about ME? I scan the classroom and do some quick calculating. There are only a few names Mrs. Godfrey hasn't chosen.

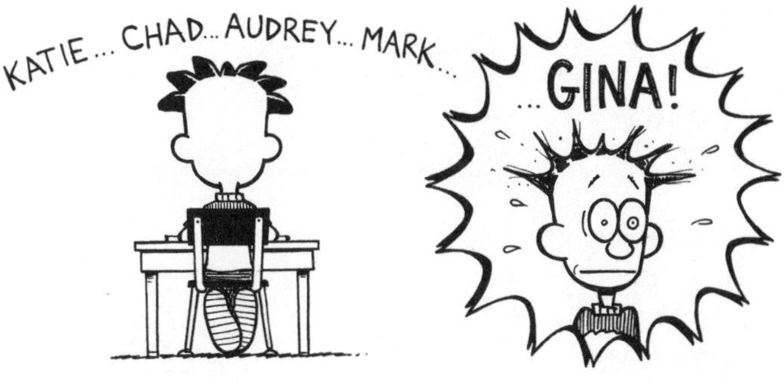
KATIE... CHAD... AUDREY... MARK...
...GINA!

My stomach does a swan dive down to my shoes. Gina hasn't been paired with anybody yet.

Oh, please, no. PLEASE don't let me get stuck with Gina. ANYONE but her.

Mrs. Godfrey reaches into the jar again.

What a RELIEF!! I'm fine with being Megan's partner. MORE than fine. Megan's pretty cool. She's nice, she's smart . . .

She's not here. Megan? Anybody seen Megan?

"Oh, wait," says Mrs. Godfrey. "I just remembered Megan's having her tonsils removed this week. She'll be absent for a while."

"B-but I don't mind waiting until Megan gets back," I stammer. "I'll just—"

"QUIET, Nate," Mrs. Godfrey barks. Before I can get another word out, she's got her hand back in the cookie jar. "You'll be working with . . ."

"Is there a PROBLEM, you two?" Mrs. Godfrey asks in a tone that makes it clear there'd better not be.

Typical Gina. She says exactly what the teacher wants to hear. But I can't pretend everything's fine and dandy when it isn't. Mrs. Godfrey's eyes look like they're about to burn a hole in my head. But she asked if there's a problem, and I'm going to give her an answer.

"Really?" she answers, sounding surprised. "Well, I can't imagine WHY!"

A few kids snicker. Mrs. Godfrey turns and starts writing on the blackboard. That's her way of telling me this conversation is over. There's no way out. I'm officially partners with Gina.

CHAPTER 3

"I'm so mad at Megan's tonsils," I grumble as Francis, Teddy, and I stop by our lockers.

"Right," says Francis. "I'm sure that was all part of Megan's master plan."

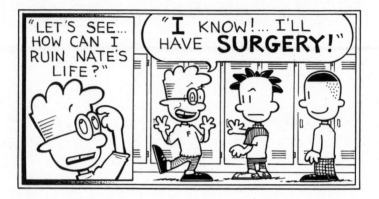

"Okay, okay," I say. "You don't have to make it sound so stupid."

"Well, Mrs. Godfrey won't let you dump Gina," Francis points out, "so you might as well make the best of it."

"Easy for YOU to say," I shoot back. "YOU'RE not the one stuck with her!"

Groan. Gina and her precious academic record. I've only heard this about a thousand times.

"You know what, Gina? I could do as well as you if I really wanted to," I tell her.

"Then why DON'T you?"

"Because," I answer, "there's more to life than good grades!"

"Listen, Einstein," Gina snarls. "When you're working with ME . . ."

"Our paper topic is Benjamin Franklin," she says slowly. "Think you can remember that?"

I don't answer. Actually, I CAN'T answer, what with Gina strangling me and all. Finally she lets me go and stalks off toward—shocker!—the library. Her home away from home.

"Mrs. Godfrey was right," Teddy teases.

I'm about to hip check him into the water fountain when . . .

"Guys!" I say excitedly. "It's TUESDAY!"

Pause.

"Congratulations," says Francis. "Did you figure that out all by yourself?"

That perks them up. We head for the gym as fast as we can. We don't run, because if you get caught running in the hallways, you get detention.

So we just walk super-fast, even though it makes you look like you need to go to the bathroom really, really bad.

Great timing. Coach is putting up the list just as we're racewalking around the corner.

INTRAMURAL FLEECEBALL CAPTAINS

1. Helen T.
2. Reed M.
3. Nate W.
4. Becky L.
5. Randy B.
6. Matt P.
7. Hannah M.
8. Peter R.

Captains will select teams AFTER SCHOOL TODAY!
— Coach Calhoun

There are two kinds of sports at P.S. 38: the official ones you play against other schools, like soccer and basketball and lacrosse; and the UNofficial ones that you play between seasons. All the teachers call them intramurals, but the kids call them SPOFFs:

S PORTS

P LAYED

O NLY

F OR

F UN

example: flag football

BONK!

I've got to be honest: They're not played ONLY for fun. You're playing against kids you've known your whole life, so it can get pretty intense. It's more than sports. It's bragging rights.

And there's a trophy.

It's the sorriest-looking thing you've ever seen. But SPOFFs are such a big deal, a long time ago somebody decided there had to be a trophy. So they wrapped some aluminum foil around an empty Dr Pepper can and called it the Spoffy, the most idiotic name for a trophy of all time.

I want to win that stupid thing so bad. I've just got to.

My SPOFF career has been a disaster so far. It's not my fault. I just keep ending up on lame teams.

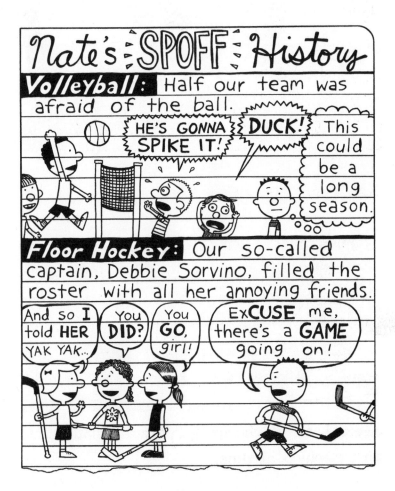

And the one time I was actually on a half-decent team?

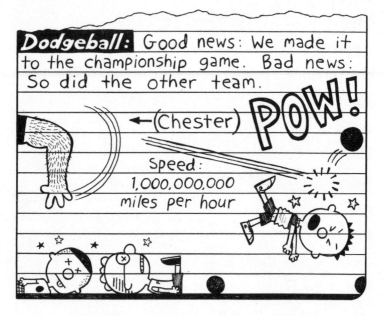

Dodgeball: Good news: We made it to the championship game. Bad news: So did the other team.

←(Chester)

POW!

Speed: 1,000,000,000 miles per hour

So obviously I've never won the Spoffy. But here's why this is my big chance. First, I'm a captain. That means I get to pick my own team! It's not random, like that cookie jar thing in social studies.

EL CAPITÁN

Second, I'm really good at fleeceball. But if you don't have fleeceball at your school, you probably have no idea what I'm talking about.

Fleeceball is indoor baseball. Most of the rules are the same, except instead of a baseball bat, you use a broom handle. The ball's puffy, so it doesn't hurt if it hits you. Last year Chad got drilled right in the face, and he was totally fine.

And one more thing: It's not a good idea to slide when you're running the bases.

"You're gonna pick me for your team, right, Nate?" asks Teddy.

"Of COURSE I am, as long as another captain doesn't pick you first," I say.

Randy's a bully. He walks around acting like he owns the school, and he's always got a posse of five or six guys trailing after him like a bunch of pilot fish. And I don't even think THEY like him. They just PRETEND to like him because they're afraid of him.

"Step aside, scrubs," he barks at us. Then he checks the list. He does a little fist pump when he sees his name.

Then he looks at it again and turns toward me.

"Coach made YOU a captain?" he says.

Is Randy trying to trash-talk me? Fine. Bring it on.

"I AM good at sports," I tell him. "But it takes more than that to be a captain."

"Like what?" he sneers.

"I'll show you," I say.

I lead Randy and his crew down the hallway. I sneak a couple of looks over my shoulder to make sure they're still with me. So far, so good.

We stop.

"What's this all about?" Randy demands.

"I told you I was going to show you an important part of being a captain," I say, turning toward my locker. "Here it is."

Randy tries to say something, but he can't. He's too busy getting crushed by the avalanche of garbage that just exploded out of my locker. I guess being a slob has its advantages.

He'll probably kill me later. And maybe his fleece-ball team will totally destroy mine. But right now, I really don't care. I went up against the biggest jerk in school, and I won.

Score!

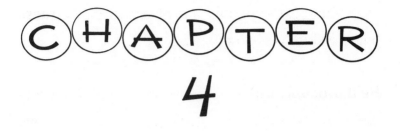

CHAPTER 4

News travels fast in middle school. It took about five seconds for the whole sixth grade to hear how I punked Randy.

Mr. Big Shot isn't used to getting laughed at. So he's probably got one thing on his mind:

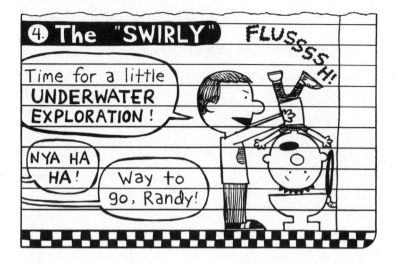

He's been looking for me all day. But he'll never find me here. I'm in the library.

I wasn't PLANNING to be in the library. Five minutes ago I was in science, my last class of the day. But then things got a little out of hand. That seems to happen to me a lot.

It started out okay. Mr. Galvin said we were doing an experiment about energy. That was funny, because Mr. Galvin and energy don't exactly go together.

ZZZZZ... magnetic fields... ZZZ... hydrochloric acid... ZZZZZZZ... argyle socks... ZZZZZ...

Anyway, we each got a little car and a board to use as a ramp. We were supposed to keep changing the angle of the ramp, and measure how far the car rolled each time.

THIS TIME, IT WENT SIX FEET!

WHOOP-DE-DOO.

Guess what? The steeper the ramp, the farther the car went. Duh. What's next, doing an experiment to prove water is wet?

The whole thing was a day trip to Camp Boredom. And then I got the idea to liven things up by customizing my car.

I turned it into the BATMOBILE! Pretty cool, right? So then I figured: Why stop there?

Yeah, it was probably a little goofy, but I was getting laughs. AND it was making science FUN for a change. Until . . .

Ever notice that teachers always ask what you're doing when anybody with half a brain could figure it out? I didn't know what Mr. Galvin wanted me to say, so I decided to go with Old Reliable:

I guess Mr. Galvin's not a big Batman fan. His jaw muscles started to twitch, which always means trouble. I expected him to launch into one of those screaming fits where his voice gets all weird and shaky. But he just gave one of those "I'm-so-disappointed-in-you" sighs and said:

The library? I didn't see THAT one coming, but, hey, fine by me. I cleaned things up, headed for the door . . .

. . . and then the other shoe dropped.

Shoot. It's bad enough getting yelled at during school hours. But getting chewed out on my OWN time?

Still, it's better than sitting in science watching Mr. Galvin's arteries harden. The library's my favorite hangout spot in school. It's perfect for table football. There are hardly ever any teachers here. And best of all . . .

I snuggle deep into the chair. Ahhhh, this is nice. I'll just relax here for a while and . . .

Oop. It's Hickey. Mrs. Hickson, I mean. She's the head librarian, and she's not really into "hanging out." I'm pretty sure the bean-bag chairs weren't her idea. If you're in her library, she wants to see you DOING something.

MRS. HICKSON FACT:
She never forgets a name, a face . . . or an overdue book.

"OLD YELLER."

"THE PHANTOM TOLLBOOTH."

"HOLES."

RETURNS

UM... YEAH, I'M DOING RESEARCH ON BEN FRANKLIN.

"Well, then," she answers, "wouldn't a BOOK come in handy?"

Librarians. Aren't they hilarious?

Great. So much for my date with the beanbag chair. Instead I'm stuck reading about some guy who's been worm food for a couple of centuries.

Except . . . you know what?

This Ben Franklin dude was actually pretty cool!

Before now, all I knew about Ben Franklin was that a) he was kind of chubby, and b) his picture is on the hundred-dollar bill. But it turns out that he did all sorts of amazing stuff back in Colonial times. Basically, the man was a genius. Like me.

I open my binder and start taking notes.

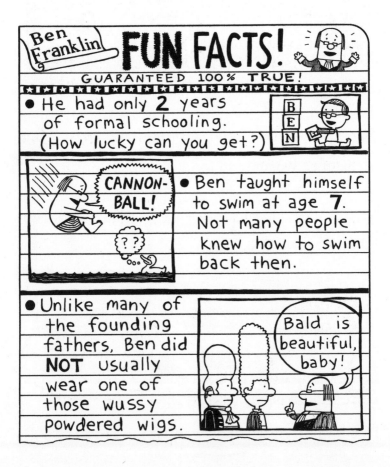

"Nate," calls Mrs. Hickson from the front desk. "The bell rang."

It did? Wow, I got so wrapped up in my work that I didn't hear a thing.

I hurry toward the science room, hoping Mr. Galvin isn't there. Maybe he went home. Maybe he forgot about me.

No such luck.

Whoa, hold on. Did he just call me a show-off? That is SO bogus. I wasn't showing off, I was just trying to make science a little more interesting. Or did

Mr. Galvin miss the fact that his little car and ramp experiment was a total yawnathon?

"School is serious business, Nate," he continues. "It's not fun and games."

Fun and games.

Oh, NO!!!

I'm supposed to be in the GYM right now! I have to pick players for my fleeceball team!!

I break into a sweat. Mr. Galvin's still flapping his gums, but I can't just stand here and wait for him to shut up.

Silence. Okay, mission accomplished. He stopped talking. But did I just make things worse?

"All right then, Nate," he says finally. "I accept your apology."

I'm out the door and on my way to the gym at about warp 10. Forget that whole "no running in the hallways" rule. This is an emergency!

"I'm afraid you're too late, Nate," Coach tells me. "The captains' meeting is over."

"Over?" I say, my heart sinking. I feel my chance to win the Spoffy slipping away. "But—"

Coach reads my mind. "Don't worry, Nate," he says with a smile. "You're still a captain. And you've got yourself a team."

For a second, I feel a little twinge of disappointment. I was really looking forward to picking the team myself. But then I start reading the roster Coach gave me.

Francis and Teddy are on my team! YES!! And there are a lot of other good players here, too!

"Wow, this team could be a POWERHOUSE!" I exclaim. "Thanks, Coach!"

BUT... AREN'T THERE SUPPOSED TO BE **TEN** KIDS PER TEAM?

THERE ARE ONLY **NINE** NAMES HERE!

Coach looks confused for a second. He glances over my shoulder.

MOVE YOUR THUMB.

I slide my thumb to the side. There, at the bottom of the list, is the tenth name. No! NO!!

I almost gag. Is this some kind of sick JOKE? What's Gina doing signing up for fleeceball? She doesn't even LIKE sports. She's going to ruin everything!

Whoa. Wait a sec. My team. MY team.

I'M the captain. I'M in charge. The other players have to do what I say. Including Gina.

Maybe this won't be so bad after all. Maybe, for once, I've got Gina right where I want her.

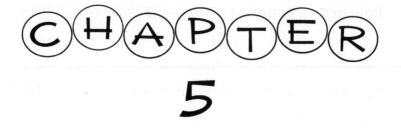

"What's our team called?" Francis asks as the three of us walk home.

"Nothing," I say.

I ignore them. "I didn't have a name ready when I talked to Coach," I explain. "So he gave me until homeroom tomorrow to come up with one."

"Well, make sure it's a GOOD one," Teddy says. "There's nothing worse than being on a team with a bad name."

Yeah, that was pretty embarrassing.

"Still, we DID have a pretty catchy slogan," Francis reminds us.

We reach my house. "Well, one season as a Hot Dog was enough," I say. "I definitely won't be giving us some stupid FOOD name."

"So we're not going to be Nate's Noodles?" Teddy asks.

"How about you clowns let an EXPERT handle this? By tomorrow I'll have the perfect team name."

"Gina's Gerbils!" Teddy calls.

"Hi, Nate," says Dad from the kitchen. "How was school?"

"Not bad," I say, my stomach rumbling. All that talk about hot dogs and tacos made me hungry.

"Sure," says Dad. "Whatever you can find."

Whatever I can find? Good one, Dad. See, our house isn't like other houses. Welcome to . . .

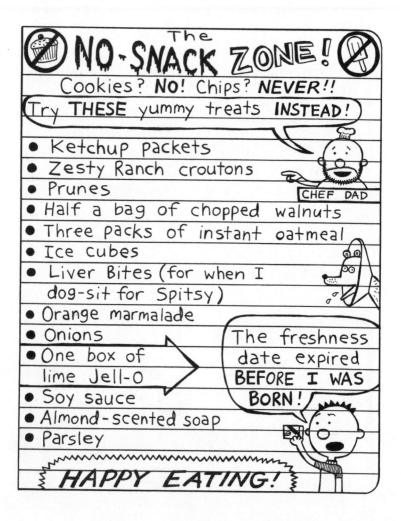

This is pathetic. Would it kill Dad to keep a few bags of Cheez Doodles lying around? I'm about to start gnawing on a table leg when . . .

Oop. That's my cue to go up to my room. I don't need to listen to Ellen blabbing away about all the boys who never notice her or what kind of lip gloss she's going to wear tomorrow.

"Who is it?" I ask.

"How should I know?" answers Ellen. She's obviously devastated that the call isn't for her.

A girl??? That hardly ever happens. The last time a girl called me, it was Annette Bingham selling Girl Scout cookies. I'm trying to figure out who it might be when a thought hits me:

How awesome would THAT be? I try to stay calm as I reach for the phone. Very cool. Very suave.

Ugh. Letdown City. Gina's voice sounds even more annoying over the phone. If that's possible.

"Have you done any Ben Franklin research yet?" she snaps.

Wait a minute, is she CHECKING UP on me? "As a matter of fact, I HAVE," I say. "Not that it's any of your business."

"Chillax, Gina. I'm not going to screw up your per-fect record."

"You'd better not," she barks. "Because any grade below an A plus would mean . . ."

The old low-battery trick. Works every time.

"Who was on the phone?" Dad asks hopefully. Uh, sorry, Dad. The only people who ever call you are telemarketers.

Thanks SO much, Ellen. Now Dad's going to get all parental on me.

"A GIRL!" he says, raising his eyebrows. "Really?"

"It wasn't a girl," I mutter. "It was Gina."

Okay, this is officially grossing me out. "NO!" I yell, almost gagging. "Gina's my ARCHENEMY!"

"Ooh!" Ellen chimes in. "Mrs. Godfrey?"

Whoops. Big mistake. I should never mention Mrs. Godfrey around Ellen, because . . .

See? The floodgates have opened. And now she's running up to her room and coming back with . . .

That's a big difference between Ellen and me. She saves her report cards. I burn mine.

Ellen sounds giddy. "Want to hear some of the comments Mrs. Godfrey gave me back then?"

"Ahem!" she begins.

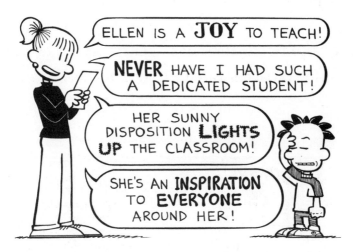

This is disgusting. I stomp up to my room. If I wanted to hear someone brag about her grades, I would have stayed on the phone with Gina.

Besides, I already knew that Mrs. Godfrey is the world's number one Ellen fan. She made that clear the night of the P.S. 38 Open House.

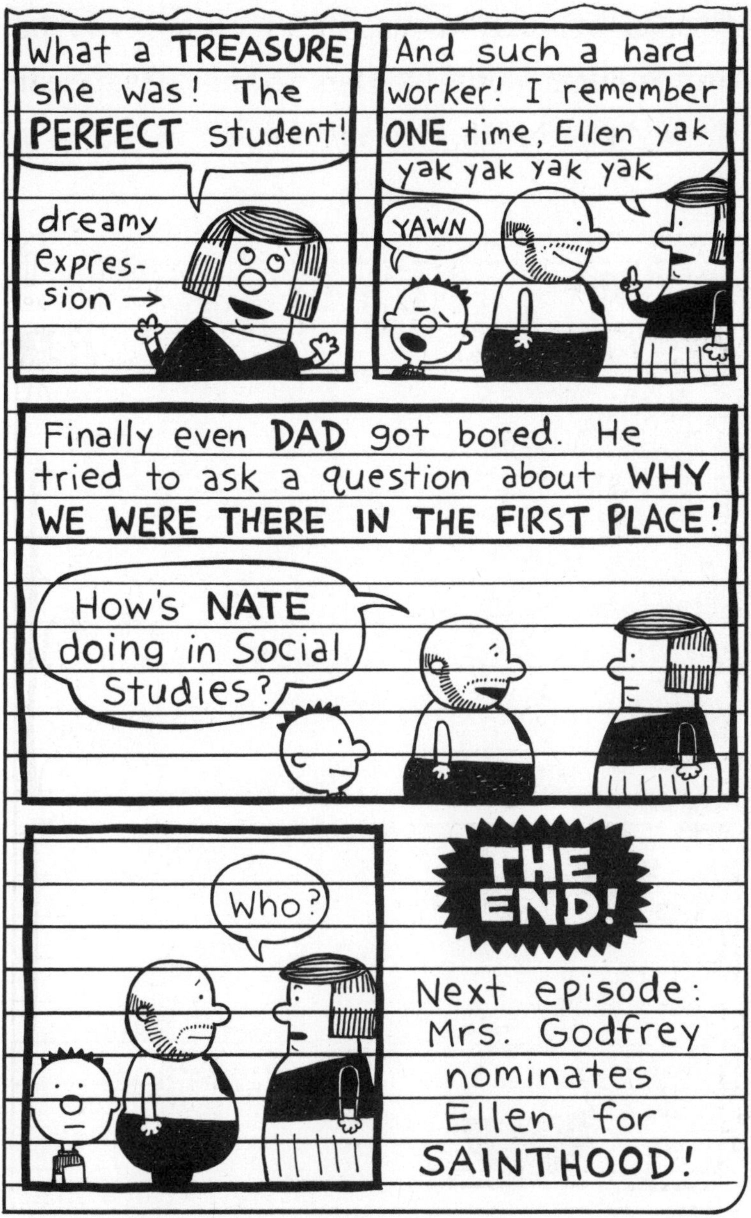

What a **TREASURE** she was! The **PERFECT** student!
dreamy expres-sion →
And such a hard worker! I remember **ONE** time, Ellen yak yak yak yak yak
YAWN
Finally even **DAD** got bored. He tried to ask a question about **WHY WE WERE THERE IN THE FIRST PLACE!**
How's **NATE** doing in Social Studies?
Who?
THE END!
Next episode: Mrs. Godfrey nominates Ellen for **SAINTHOOD!**

Don't get me wrong. It's not that I really WANT Mrs. Godfrey to like me. The kids she likes are all a bunch of dweebs. But sixth grade would be a lot easier for me . . .

...IF **ELLEN** HADN'T BEEN THERE FIRST.

Okay, enough about Ellen. Thanks to her little Me-Fest—and Gina's phone call—I haven't had time to focus on what's REALLY important:

WHAT SHOULD I NAME MY FLEECE-BALL TEAM?

I need a name that stands out. A lot of kids name their SPOFF teams after their favorite pro team. What's fun about THAT? Where's the imagination? I want to come up with something ORIGINAL.

I grab a pencil. Time to start brainstorming.

Potential **TEAM NAMES**

from the brilliant mind of
CAPTAIN NATE WRIGHT!

- Fleece Police
- Wrecking Balls
- Spoffy Or Die
- No Mercy
- Grave Diggers
- Broom Handle Bombers
- Gym Rats
- Going, Going, Gone!
- Wall Bangers
- The Wright Stuff
- We're Champs, You're Chumps
- Bring The Pain
- Power Up
- Losing Is Not An Option
- Nate-orious

POW!

NAB!

Hmm. These are good, but none of 'em are knocking my socks off.

Holy cow! Is that SPITSY?

Spitsy belongs to our neighbor Mr. Eustis, and compared to other dogs, he's sort of lame. He wears a ridiculous purple sweater and a halo collar that makes him look like a walking satellite dish. He has a knack for jumping on you right after he's been rolling around in something dead. And one time, he infested my backpack with fleas.

But he's never LOUD. I run to the window to see what's got him so freaked out. Looks like Spitsy's barking at . . .

. . . nothing.

Maybe something WAS there a second ago. Maybe he saw a cat, or maybe a squirrel ran by. I can't see anything now. But Spitsy's still going completely psycho.

Hey! That's IT!

Remember how I said I wanted my team to stand out? Well, this is just the name to do it. It's perfect. I can't wait to tell the guys.

They'll be crazy about it.

CHAPTER 6

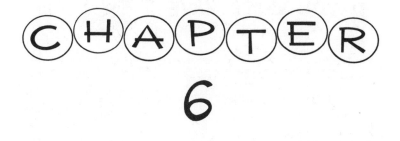

I was right. When I tell Francis and Teddy that we're going to be the Psycho Dogs, they're totally into it. So the day's off to a great start.

Oop. That didn't last long.

Chad's right. As we get closer to the school yard, I can see Randy and his little gang of sidekicks hanging out by the tetherball pole. You don't have to be Einstein to figure out his plan.

But no need to panic. I've got the school yard safety policy on my side.

I don't think they even HAD a safety policy until last year. But then came the Eric Fleury Incident.

Eric's completely obsessed with martial arts stuff. He'll be doing something normal, like standing in the lunch line. And then, for no reason, he'll break into a bunch of kung fu moves. Weird.

One day during recess, Eric and Danny DelFino were play fighting in the school yard, doing kick-boxing and karate and stuff. It was sort of a dork fest, but I have to admit: It looked pretty real.

I guess it looked a little TOO real. Principal Nichols had no clue they were just messing around.
He started running toward them. And he almost NEVER runs, not even in the kids versus teachers basketball game.

When they saw him charging at them like a runaway hippo, it must have messed up their super kung fu concentration. They both sort of fell down.

Eric landed funny. You could hear the snap all the way over by the parking lot. He broke his arm.

Of course after that the school went totally over-board. They outlawed play fighting and just about anything else that's fun. Which makes for some pretty boring recesses.

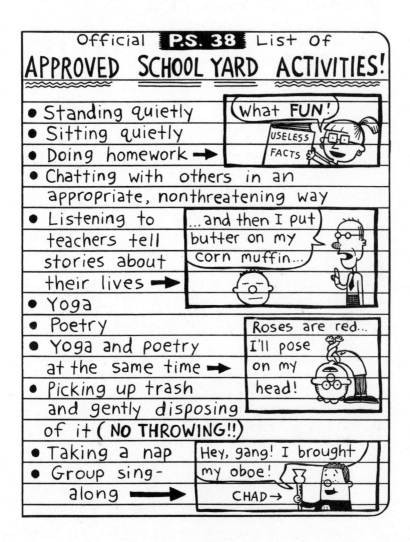

Official **P.S. 38** List of
APPROVED SCHOOL YARD ACTIVITIES!

- Standing quietly
- Sitting quietly
- Doing homework →
- Chatting with others in an appropriate, nonthreatening way
- Listening to teachers tell stories about their lives →
- Yoga
- Poetry
- Yoga and poetry at the same time →
- Picking up trash and gently disposing of it (**NO THROWING!!**)
- Taking a nap
- Group sing-along →

What **FUN!**

USELESS FACTS

...and then I put butter on my corn muffin...

Roses are red...
I'll pose on my head!

Hey, gang! I brought my oboe!

CHAD →

But you know what? Right now I'm FINE with the safety policy, because it's going to keep Randy off my back. If he tries anything that even LOOKS like we're fighting, the playground patrol will be all over him. So I'm not worried.

Until I see who's on duty.

Coach John's old-school. I'm pretty sure he doesn't care much about the safety policy. He's always telling us we need a little LESS safety.

If he sees Randy mopping the asphalt with my face, he'll probably just let it happen. He'll say it's good character building.

So I can't count on Coach John to bail me out. And I bet Randy knows it, too. As we walk onto the school yard, he and his posse don't even try to hide the fact they're about to ambush me. I've got a feeling I'm about to replace Eric Fleury as the poster child for school-yard injuries. I can hear it now: Remember the Nate Wright Incident?

Then I get a brilliant idea.

I've got a head start on Randy, but not a big one. And this backpack is slowing me down. I can feel him gaining on me as I motor across the school yard and into the building.

Principal Nichols! Looks like he forgot to take his happy pill this morning.

Recreation? Excuse me, I was running for my LIFE! But I can't say that with Randy standing only two feet away.

Principal Nichols isn't buying it.

I nod, and so does Randy. I guess he wants to stick close to me, what with him wanting to kill me and all.

"Well, then, you BOTH must know the answer to this question . . . "

What was the name of the popular book that Ben Franklin published every year from 1732 to 1758?

"'Poor Richard's Almanack,'" I say immediately.

The Big Guy looks kind of surprised. Maybe even impressed. "Very well, Nate," he says. "You may go to the computer lab."

Whew. That was close. Randy shuffles away, look-ing even MORE like he wants to kill me. I scoot into the lab before Principal Nichols can slap any more Ben Franklin questions on me.

Speaking of Ben, I wonder if he ever had to deal with jerks like Randy?

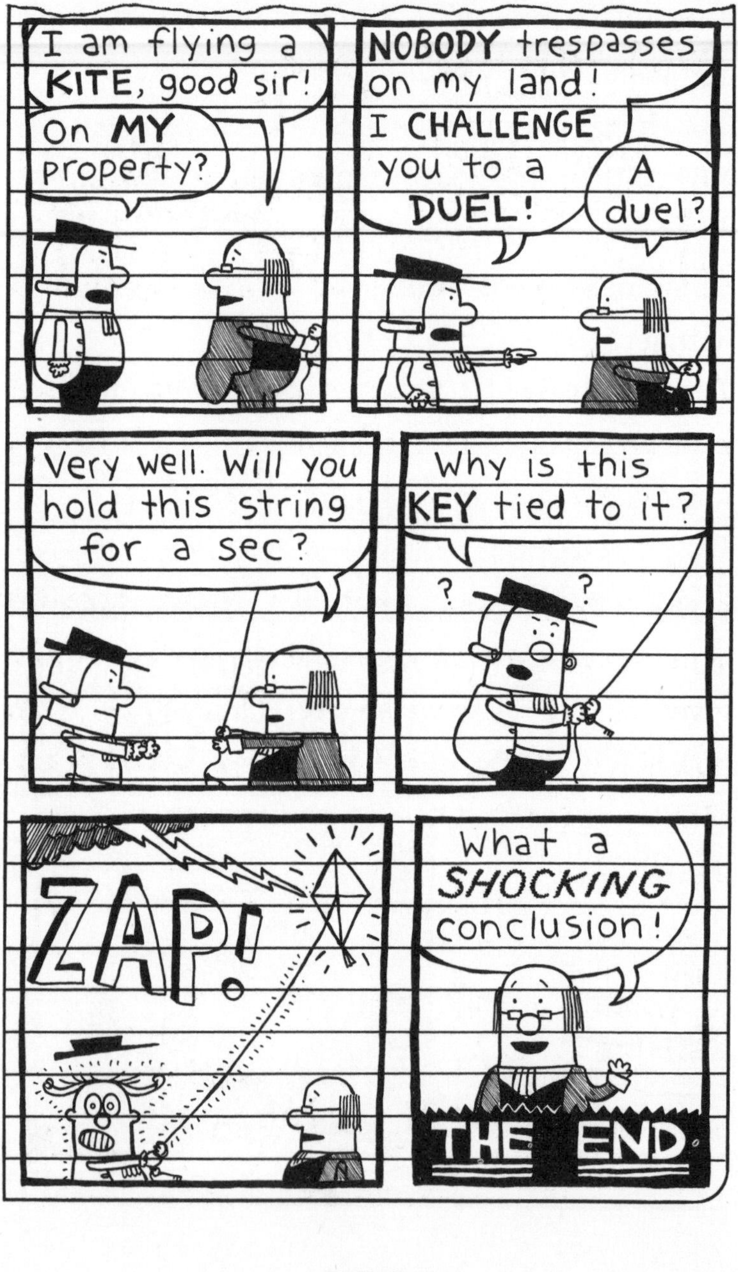
I am flying a KITE, good sir!
On MY property?
NOBODY trespasses on my land! I CHALLENGE you to a DUEL!
A duel?
Very well. Will you hold this string for a sec?
Why is this KEY tied to it?
? ?
ZAP!
What a SHOCKING conclusion!
THE END.

There's the bell. I head for homeroom, making sure to avoid Randy. Once classes start, I can sort of relax. He's not in any of my sections.

It's a pretty typical morning. Mrs. Godfrey screams at me a couple of times in social studies. Ms. Clarke gives us some new vocab words in English. (Hey, how about "extremely" and "boring"?) And in art, Mr. Rosa lets us make clay sculptures.

"A WALRUS??" I say. "It's a PSYCHO DOG, you moron!"

"Uh-oh, what?" I ask, still a little peeved.

"Did you remember to tell Coach our team name this morning?" Francis asks.

Coach wanted that name by homeroom! I was so worried about getting away from Randy, I totally forgot!

How stupid can I get? I hope Coach wasn't too mad when I didn't show up.

Finally the bell rings. Thirty seconds later, I'm at his office door.

"Sorry I didn't give you the name of my fleeceball team this morning," I stammer. "I was—"

Coach interrupts me with a friendly smile. "No problem, Nate," he says.

Wait a minute. How'd THAT happen? "You . . . you did?" I ask.

"Right on time . . . ," he says.

Did he say . . . GINA?? The room starts spinning. I open my mouth to speak, but nothing comes out.

"I'm proud of you for letting her pick the name, Nate," Coach continues.

"Wait!" I say as he walks out. "What did Gina . . . ?"

"I printed up the schedule. There are copies on my file cabinet," he calls back to me.

I'm afraid to look.

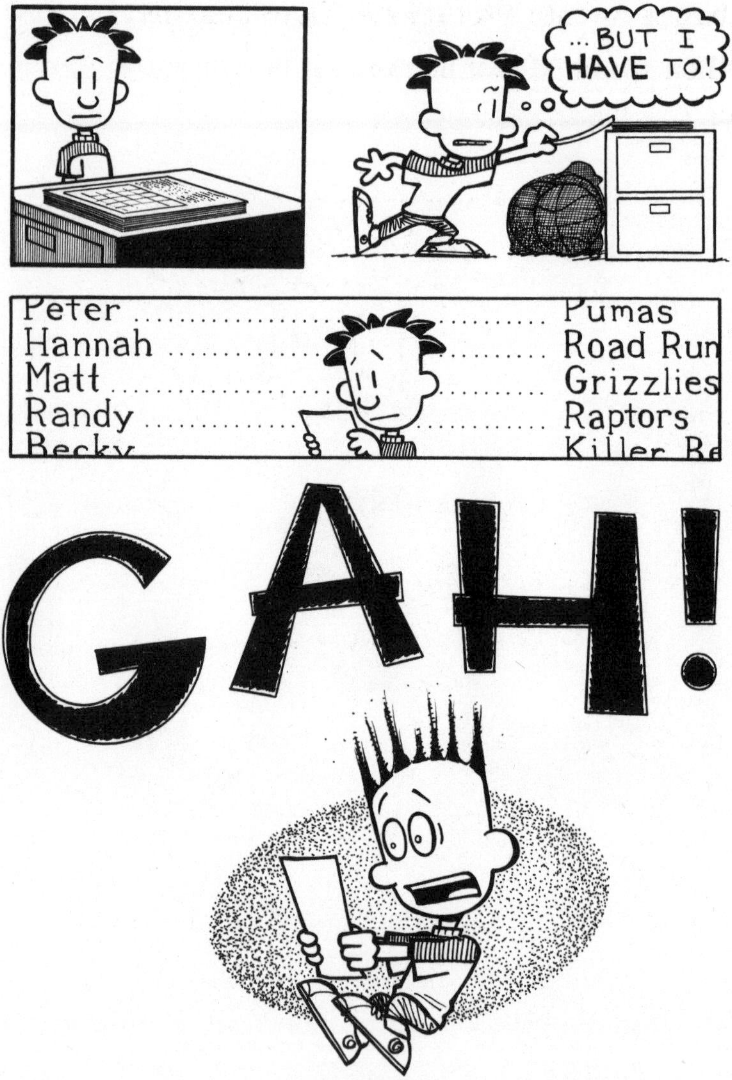
...BUT I HAVE TO!
Peter .... Pumas
Hannah .... Road Run
Matt .... Grizzlies
Randy .... Raptors
GAH!

It's worse than I thought. Worse than ANYBODY could have thought. Gina just turned my fleece-ball team into a total joke. Thanks to her, I'm now the captain of a bunch of . . .

CHAPTER 7

I don't care what the schedule says. I'm still going to call us the Psycho Dogs.

But nobody else is.

> **HEY!** IT'S THE CAPTAIN OF THE **KUDDLE KITTENS!**

Great. Coach already posted the schedule. Half the school's seen it by now, and the other half's checking it out on the way into the lunchroom. What a disaster.

Oh, how I hate her. I don't know how she convinced Coach to let her name the team. But I do know she won't get away with it.

Remember my Things I Can't Stand list? Egg salad is on it. So obviously I'm not going to EAT this slop. I have other plans for it.

I do a quick scan of the tables and spot Gina right away. She's sitting near the stage with her pals from the big brain society. Ugh. Look at that stuck-up smile on her face. Okay, Gina, let's see if you're still smiling . . .

I can make it look like an accident. I'll act like I'm on my way to the vending machines, and then my tray will somehow "slip" out of my hands. HA!

Everything stops. The whole lunchroom goes quiet. Until Jenny starts screaming at me.

She's not just mad. She's GODFREY mad. Her eyes look like they could burn a hole in my forehead. She scrapes some of the egg salad out of her hair, and for a second I think she's going to throw it at me. Then Coach shows up.

Mess. That's a pretty good word to describe my day. First Randy goes after me. Then Gina wussifies my fleeceball team. And now Jenny will probably never talk to me again.

Okay, she's still talking to me. So it's not all bad.

I finish cleaning up and find Francis and Teddy.

"This afternoon?"

"Uh, hello? Fleeceball captain?" Francis says. "Our first game's TODAY!"

"And speaking of fleeceball," Teddy says . . .

I tell them the whole story. They're not surprised. They know what a pain Gina is.

YES! We play the scribble game all the time. It's pretty simple: Somebody makes a scribble . . .

. . . and then you have to turn that scribble into something.

It's a blast. We're just getting warmed up when . . .

Great. Artur. He's probably ticked off that I dumped egg salad all over Jenny.

"Hallo, guys," he says, smiling. Hm. Guess not. Artur probably doesn't even GET mad. He's too perfect for that.

"Sure!" say Francis and Teddy together. I sort of shrug. Whatever.

Don't get me wrong. I like Artur okay. But it's sort of annoying how nothing ever goes wrong for him. He's never been chased all over the school by Randy. He's never played "drop the lunch tray" with the whole school watching . . . because he's . . .

"Here, Artur," says Teddy, handing him a scribble.

"Better hurry, Artur," Francis says. "The bell rings in two minutes!"

One minute and fifty-nine seconds later:

Holy cow, he drew THAT in two minutes?

"That's AMAZING, Artur!" exclaims Francis.

Yeah, yeah. Let's all stand up and cheer for the amazing Artur. What's he gonna do next, discover a cure for cancer during study hall?

RRRRINNNGG!!

NATE! TODAY AFTER SCHOOL WILL BE **FUN**, YES?

HM?

TRASH

"I am on Becky's fleeceball team. We are to playing yours," he says.

YES! "Oh, really?" I say casually. "Yeah, that'll be fun."

The afternoon's a total snoozeathon—Mr. Galvin busts me for snoring during science—but somehow I make it through. The day's finally over.

Coach goes over a few ground rules (can we move this along, please?) and then the teams split up. "Okay, Psycho Dogs," I call out. "Huddle up!"

"Psycho Dogs?" says Paige.

"Wait, what is THAT thing?" I ask, looking at the lopsided ball of fur in Gina's hand.

I don't know how much more of this I can take.
Gina named us after her STUFFED CAT??

Somebody get me a bucket. I'm going to barf.

Coach blows his whistle. "Okay, Killer Bees and
Kuddle Kittens," he says . . .

Once the game starts, it doesn't matter WHAT our name is. We PLAY like Psycho Dogs. With Teddy, Francis, and me in the middle of our lineup, we score a bunch of runs right away.

But the other team keeps chipping away at our lead. Not because they're any good, but because they keep hitting the ball to Gina.

She can't catch, she can't throw, she can't hit, she can't run.

Other than that, she's great.

I'd love to sit her on the bench for the whole game. But you can't do that in SPOFFs. Everybody has to play the same amount.

In the fifth inning, she commits four errors. FOUR ERRORS!! I'm getting madder and madder. Does she even CARE? Is she even TRYING??

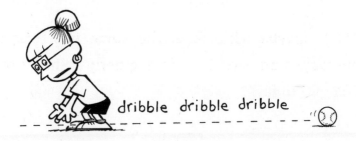

dribble dribble dribble

"Time out," calls Coach as he walks over to me. Then he lowers his voice.

"Well, maybe Gina feels the same way when she makes an error," he says quietly. "She's not TRYING to fail."

I feel my cheeks getting warm. "I know," I say.

"A captain ENCOURAGES his teammates." Coach gives me a smile that makes me feel lousy and good at the same time. The game starts up again.

So what happens? Artur (who else?) gets a lucky bloop hit with the bases loaded. Suddenly we're losing, 9–8. We're down to our last at bats. And Gina's leading off the inning.

She strikes out for the fourth time today. I bite my tongue. Teddy gets a double, so the tying run's on base. But then Francis hits an easy pop-up. Two outs.

And I'm up.

I crush the very first pitch, but it's a foul ball. The second one's right over the plate, and I take a huge hack at it.

That's two strikes. But that's okay. All it takes is one pitch. One swing can tie this game. Or win it.

It's weird: I don't feel nervous at all. I feel totally calm. I wait as the pitcher goes into his windup, watch as the ball leaves his hand. Before the ball's halfway to me, I know I'm going to hit it.

I grip the broom handle as tight as I can . . .

. . . and swing.

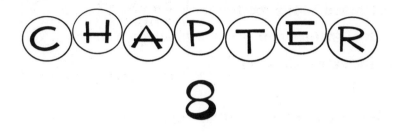

CHAPTER 8

"Is there something bothering you, Nate?" asks Dad.

Huh? Oh. Yeah, there's something bothering me. Right here on my plate.

I don't say that, though. When it comes to his cooking, Dad's not a big fan of constructive criticism. Besides, he probably knows it's not really the broccoli that's bumming me out.

"It'll help to talk about it," he says, putting on his best concerned-parent face.

I just shake my head. No offense, Big Guy, but I'm not really in the mood for one of those father-son talks. Not because I don't feel like talking. Because I don't feel like LISTENING.

> **DAD FACT:**
> *His concerned-parent face is exactly the same as his I-don't-know-how-to-work-the-DVD-player face.*

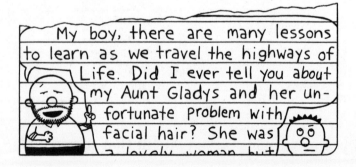

I hide the rest of my broccoli under my napkin. "May I be excused?"

Dad finally realizes I'm not going to spill my guts. He gives a little shrug and says, "Yes, you may."

 I guess it's nice of him to wonder what's going on. I mean, plenty of parents wouldn't even ASK, right?

But I just don't feel like telling him about that fleeceball game.

I was so sure I was going to hit that stupid ball.

...AND I WOULD HAVE...

...IF IT HADN'T BEEN FOR GINA!

DRAMATIC FLASHBACK

Have you ever been in The Zone? It's not a place. It's a FEELING. It's being 100 percent positive that something is about to happen exactly the way you want it to.

As the ball flew toward me, I was in The Zone. Everything was moving in super slow motion. I was totally focused. I knew what I had to do.

And then . . .

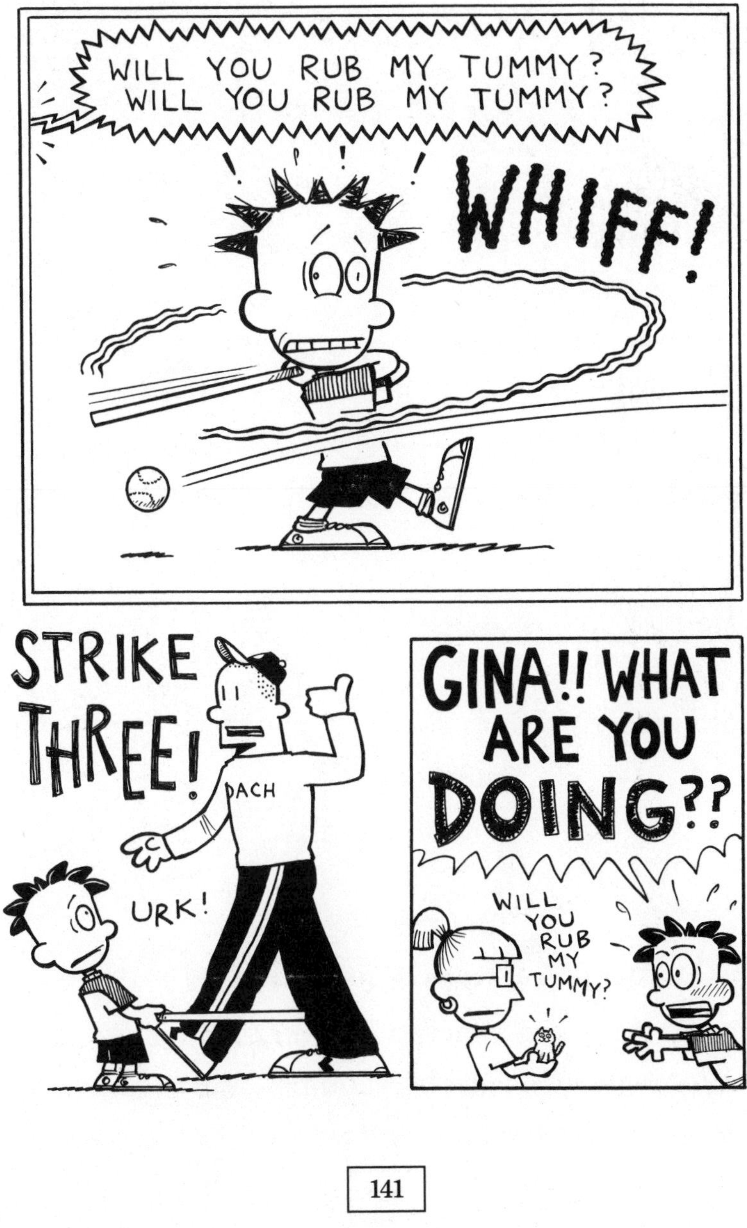
WILL YOU RUB MY TUMMY? WILL YOU RUB MY TUMMY?
WHIFF!
STRIKE THREE!
URK!
GINA!! WHAT ARE YOU DOING??
WILL YOU RUB MY TUMMY?

Coach shook his head. "Sorry, Nate," he said. "You can't call interference on your own teammate."

Game over. What a brutal ending. I wanted to take Gina's stuffed cat and rip it into a zillion pieces.

But I didn't. I just gritted my teeth and went through the handshake line.

Losing's bad enough. But when you strike out to end the game—even if it's not your fault!—that's the only thing people remember. There's nothing you can do. You're the goat.

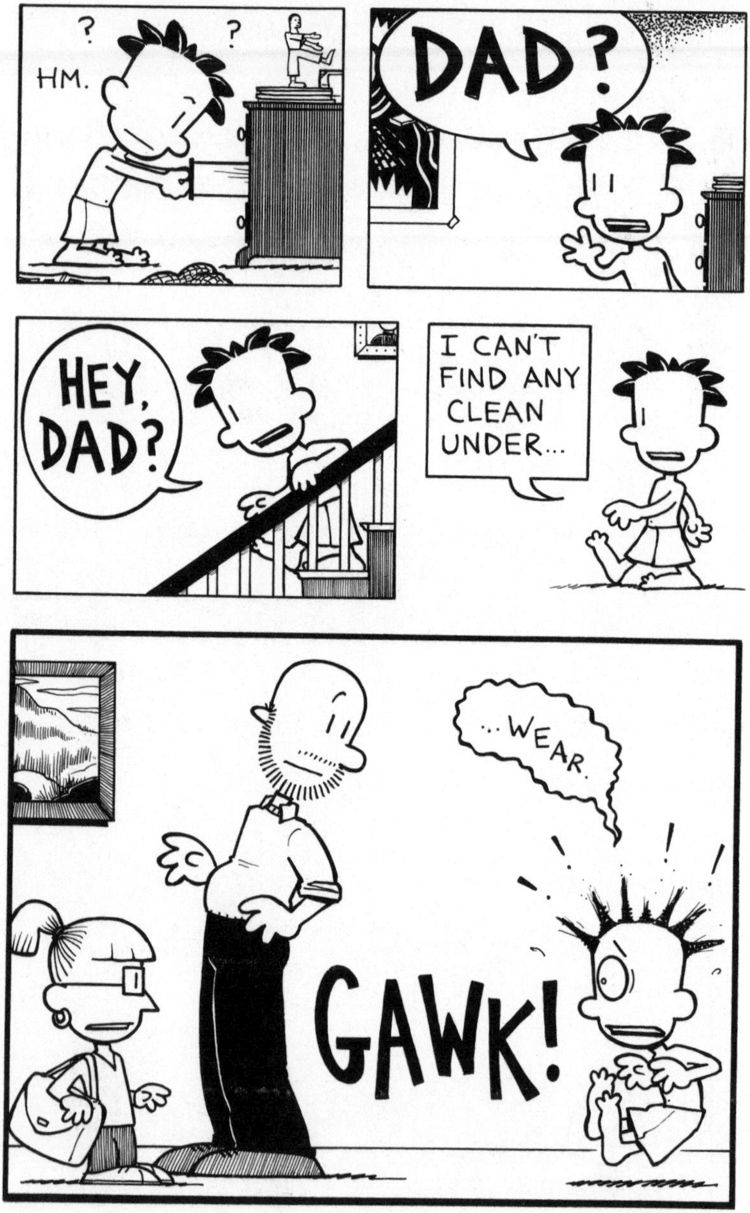

? ?
HM.
DAD?
HEY, DAD?
I CAN'T FIND ANY CLEAN UNDER...
...WEAR.
GAWK!

"Nate, your friend Gina is here," Dad says.

Oh, really??? Hey, Dad, thanks for the news flash. Did you ever think of telling me that BEFORE I came downstairs practically butt naked?

I zip down to the basement, my face burning. In half a minute I'm dressed and back in the kitchen. Dad's still Mr. Cheery.

Entertain her? What am I, a clown? How about I just find out what she wants and get RID of her?

"Oh, and Nate," Dad whispers . . .

What? CUTE? No, no, no. A puppy is cute. JENNY is cute. Gina is absolutely, positively 100 percent NOT cute.

I'll set him straight later. Right now I have to find something out:

"What do you THINK, brainless?" snarls Gina in her usual charming way. "We're doing a project together. We need to compare notes!"

She pulls out a binder the size of a suitcase and opens it up. It's exactly what you'd expect from Gina. Pages and pages of Ben Franklin research. TYPED. Footnotes. Time lines. I think I even saw a pie chart in there.

"HOLD IT!" she says. "I want to look at YOUR work!"

She smirks. How obnoxious can you get?

"I've done PLENTY of work, Gina," I tell her coldly. "Wait here."

I go up to my room and grab my folder. So she thinks she's the ONLY one who knows anything about Ben Franklin?

I slap my stuff down on the table.

It's pretty impressive, if I do say so myself. There's a little bit of everything here: awesome drawings of major events in Ben's life . . .

explanations of his amazing inventions . . .

. . . and the REAL story behind some of Ben's famous quotes.

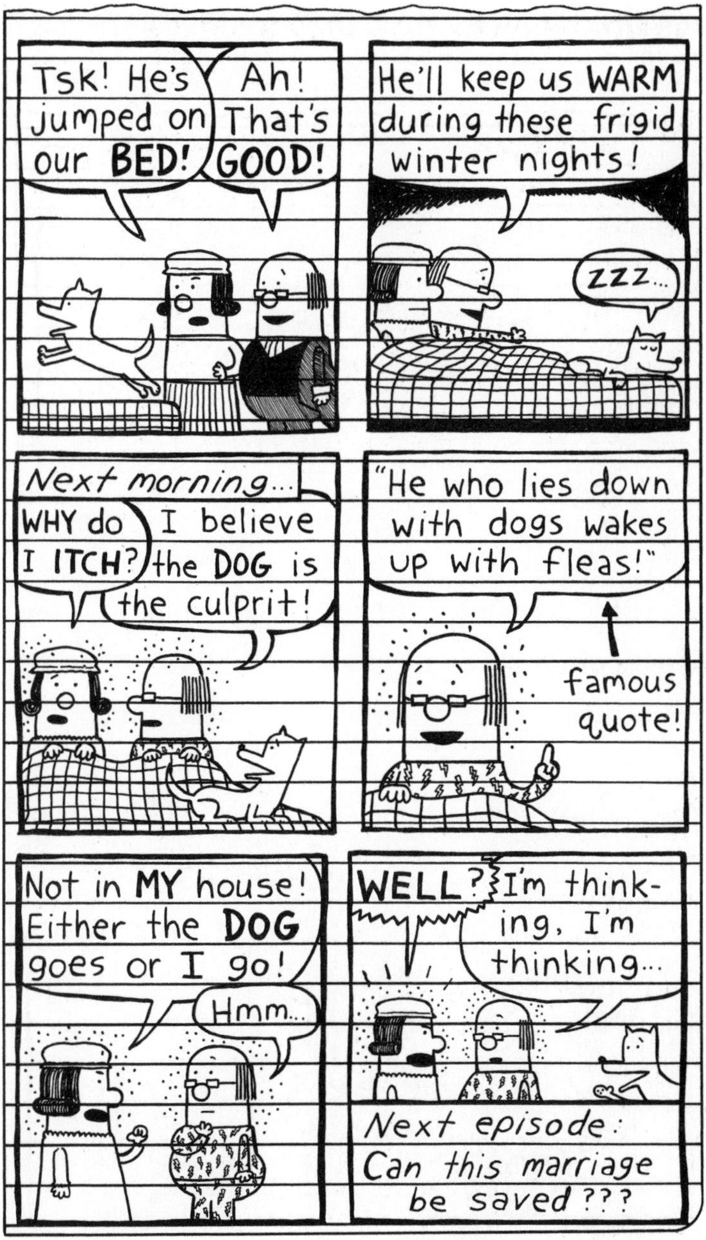
Tsk! He's jumped on our BED!
Ah! That's GOOD!
He'll keep us WARM during these frigid winter nights!
ZZZ...
Next morning...
WHY do I ITCH?
I believe the DOG is the culprit!
"He who lies down with dogs wakes up with fleas!"
famous quote!
Not in MY house! Either the DOG goes or I go!
Hmm...
WELL?
I'm think-ing, I'm thinking...
Next episode: Can this marriage be saved???

Gina barely looks at it, then gives a little snort. "Is this a JOKE?" she says. "We're not putting CARTOONS in our report!"

"If you stick these dumb drawings in my report, you'll ruin my A plus average!" she whines.

"Oh, really?"

"I don't even want to play on your stupid team!" she shouts.

I yell right back at her.

Gina thinks for a second. "Okay," she says. "I won't . . ."

"YOUR report?" I say. "Mrs. Godfrey told us to work TOGETHER."

"No problem," she says. "I'll do the report, but I'll put both our names on it."

I've got to admit, this is sounding like a pretty good plan. "And you'll quit the fleeceball team?" I ask.

"You can't just quit SPOFFs for no reason," she reminds me.

"Well, you're the brainiac, Gina," I tell her.

"Fine." She nods. "It's a deal."

He sets the tray down and flashes us a sappy smile.
Wait, does he think that . . . ?

"You weren't interrup—" I start to say.

"You two just keep on doing . . . well, whatever it is you're doing." He chuckles.

CHAPTER 9

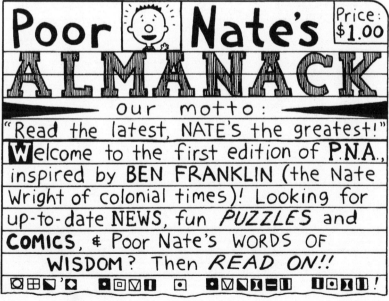

Poor Nate's

ALMANACK

Price: $1.00

our motto:

"Read the latest, NATE'S the greatest!"

Welcome to the first edition of P.N.A., inspired by BEN FRANKLIN (the Nate Wright of colonial times)! Looking for up-to-date NEWS, fun *PUZZLES* and **COMICS**, & Poor Nate's WORDS OF WISDOM? Then *READ ON!!*

TOP STORY →

SPECIAL PROJECT DUE, STUDENTS FREAK OUT

As we all know, four weeks ago, Mrs. Godfrey assigned a special project. Well, it's **DUE TOMORROW!** Some students (like yours truly) have nothing to worry about, but **OTHERS** are **PANICKING!** Here's what some of them said during a P.N.A. ***EXCLUSIVE INTERVIEW!***

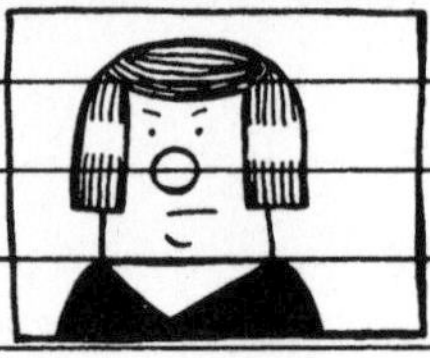

EXCLUSIVE INTERVIEW!

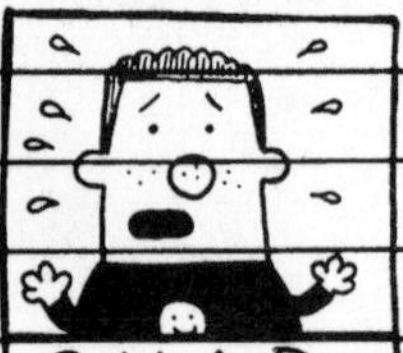

CHAD

I heard that last year, Mrs. Godfrey **FAILED** a whole bunch of kids!

This project has left me **PHYSICALLY** and **EMOTIONALLY** ***EXHAUSTED!!***

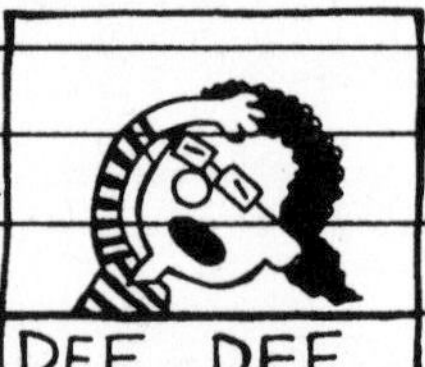

DEE DEE

Note: member of the Drama Club

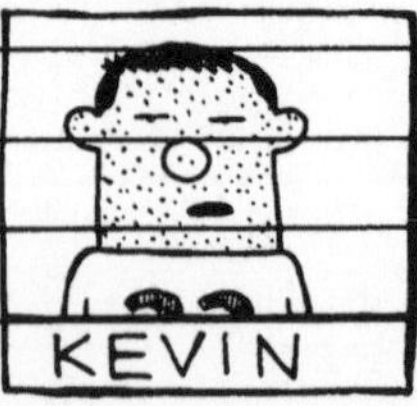

KEVIN

I have broken out in some sort of bizarre, stress-induced rash.

SOME kids have asked ~~Godzilla~~ Mrs. Godfrey for an extension. **BUT**...

SHARON: ...she just smiled and said: **NO EXTENSIONS, NO EXCEPTIONS!**

Hey, **CALM DOWN**, everybody! Remember, Ben Franklin never even **MADE** it to sixth grade... and look how awesome **HE** turned out!

* * * * * * * * * *

POOR NATE PROVERB:
"Why stress out and overwork
When your teacher's such a jerk?"

And now let's see what's going on...
◨◫◧▨◇ ◆◪◫ ◉◺◫◸◱◉!
It's time for

CLASSROOM CHATTER!

DID YOU KNOW that you can learn all kinds of private info and juicy gossip by hanging around out- side the teachers' lounge? It's **TRUE!** I recently did just that, and **HERE'S** what I overheard:

FACULTY

...and so then I him that he'd be not even THINK acting as if he even know wha TALKING ab♪

- Coach John is having some minor health problems.

- Ms. Clarke has decided to stop computer dating.

- Mr. Rosa is sort of burned out.

- Mr. Galvin is very, very boring.

TAKE HIS ADVICE or PAY THE PRICE!

ETHAN R. TWIG!

Who **IS** this *MYSTERY COLUMNIST*?

DEAR ETHAN: In Math, I sit in front of a kid whose nose whistles when he breathes. I can't

hear anything Mr. Staples says! What can I do??

Signed,
Perplexed

DEAR PERPLEXED: Don't worry that you can't hear Mr. Staples. You're not missing anything. **ANSWER TO YOUR PROBLEM**:

WHO THREW THAT?
I did!

Throw a paper airplane at Mr. Staples. He'll get mad and move your desk to the front of the room, far away from Nose Flute Boy. ***PROBLEM SOLVED!!***

Answer to Mystery:

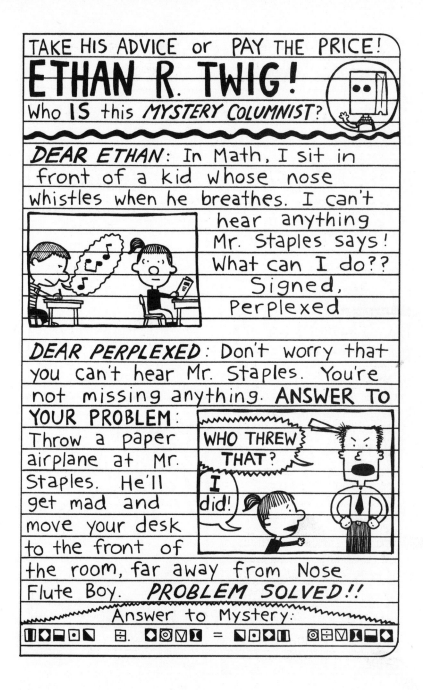

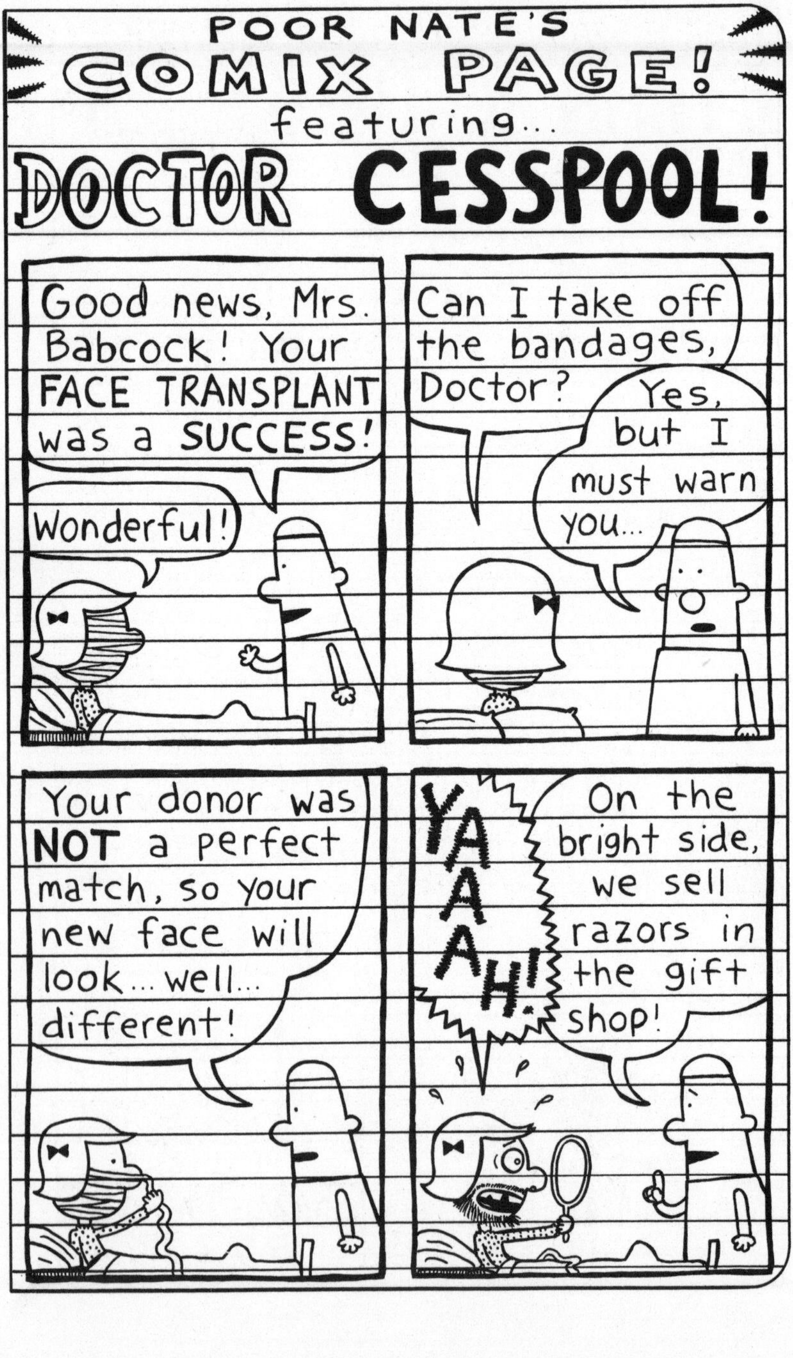
POOR NATE'S
COMIX PAGE!
featuring...
DOCTOR CESSPOOL!
Good news, Mrs. Babcock! Your FACE TRANSPLANT was a SUCCESS!
Wonderful!
Can I take off the bandages, Doctor?
Yes, but I must warn you...
Your donor was NOT a perfect match, so your new face will look... well... different!
YAAAAH!
On the bright side, we sell razors in the gift shop!

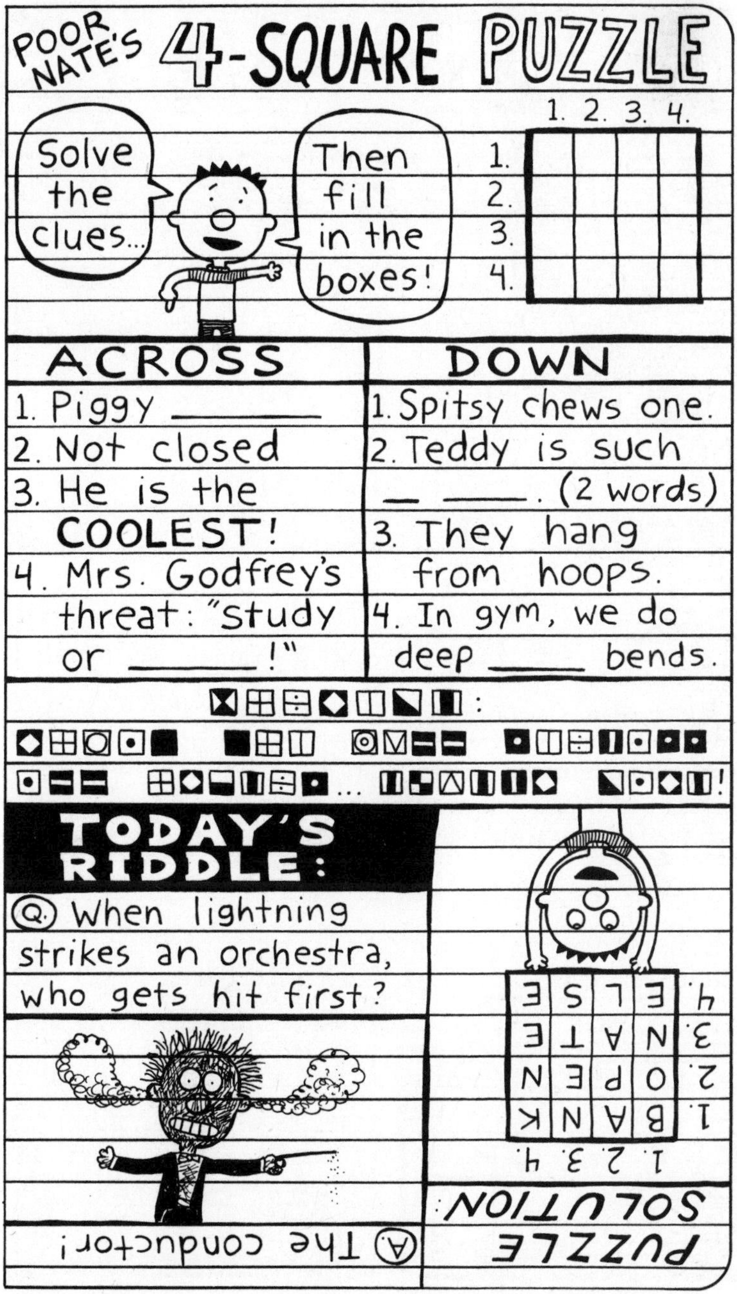
POOR NATE'S 4-SQUARE PUZZLE
Solve the clues...
Then fill in the boxes!
1. 2. 3. 4.
1.
2.
3.
4.
ACROSS
1. Piggy ______
2. Not closed
3. He is the COOLEST!
4. Mrs. Godfrey's threat: "Study or ______!"
DOWN
1. Spitsy chews one.
2. Teddy is such __ ____. (2 words)
3. They hang from hoops.
4. In gym, we do deep ____ bends.
TODAY'S RIDDLE:
Q. When lightning strikes an orchestra, who gets hit first?
A. The conductor!
PUZZLE SOLUTION:
1. 2. 3. 4.
1. B A N K
2. O P E N
3. N A T E
4. E L S E

SPOTLIGHT ON SPOFFS

The fleeceball season got off to a horrible start for the Kuddle Kittens (**real** name: Psycho Dogs) when they lost to the Killer Bees, 9-8. But led by dynamic team captain *NATE WRIGHT*, the KK's put that game behind them. They have not lost **SINCE!**

☛ *HIGHLIGHTS* of the *SEASON* ☚

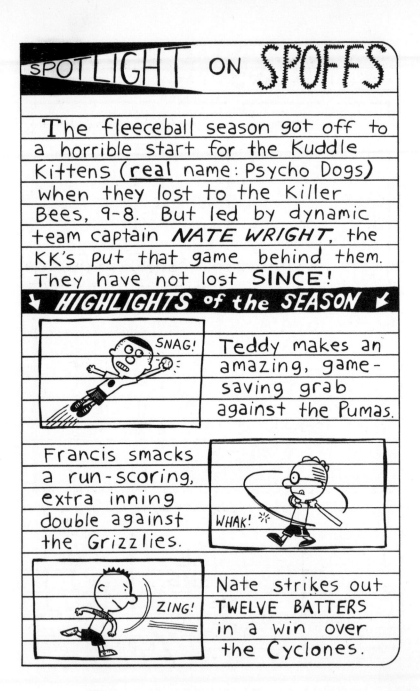

SNAG!

Teddy makes an amazing, game-saving grab against the Pumas.

Francis smacks a run-scoring, extra inning double against the Grizzlies.

WHAK!

ZING!

Nate strikes out TWELVE BATTERS in a win over the Cyclones.

And we **crush** the Chargers in fleeceball... **AND** trash-talking!

Your team didn't **DESERVE** to win! You got **LUCKY**!
If it hadn't been
and YAK
YAK YAK YAK YAK

"Well **DONE** is better than well **SAID**."
↑ Ben Franklin quote

CURRENT FLEECEBALL STANDINGS

TEAM	WINS-LOSSES
1. Kuddle Kittens	5 - 1
2. Raptors	5 - 1
3. Grizzlies	4 - 3
4. Chargers	4 - 3
5. Pumas	3 - 4
6. Cyclones	3 - 4
7. Killer Bees	3 - 4
8. Road Runners	0 - 7

There's only ***ONE GAME LEFT!***

captain:
N. Wright

KUDDLE KITTENS VS. RAPTORS

captain:
R. **BUTT**ancourt

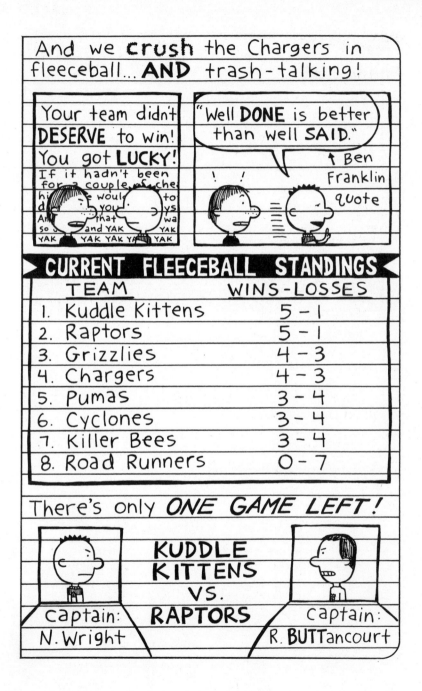

"You're asking people to pay you a DOLLAR for this?" asks Francis as he flips through a copy of "Poor Nate's Almanack."

"Yup," I answer proudly.

Francis rolls his eyes.

"I think you should add a horoscope to the next edition," Teddy says, "so people can read their fortunes."

Uh-oh. Principal Nichols. How come he's roaming around the hallways? Is somebody giving away free doughnuts?

"I'm selling an almanac," I tell him. "I'm a writer, a publisher, and a businessman! . . ."

...JUST LIKE THE SUBJECT OF MY SPECIAL PROJECT, **BEN FRANKLIN!**

See how I tied it in with the whole social studies thing? Is that smart or what?

"I admire your initiative, Nate," he says.

...BUT YOU CAN'T SELL YOUR ALMANACS DURING SCHOOL HOURS.

WAIT, **WHAT?**

"But people sell stuff in school all the TIME!" I protest.

The cheerleaders sell t-shirts...

BE A BOBCAT BOOSTER!

The science club sells candy bars...

It's the calcium phosphate that makes it yummy!

? ?

"They're doing that to raise money for specific school activities," Principal Nichols says. "What are YOU raising money for?"

UH...THE NATE WRIGHT ALLOWANCE FUND? HA HA!...

HEH... HEH... ✶GULP!✶

ONLY $1.00

POOR NATE'S ALMANACK

Nothing. Not even a smile. Hey, remember that NICE principal who handed out juice boxes on the first day of school? Whatever happened to THAT guy?

"You may do business on your OWN time, Nate," he says sternly.

He walks off, probably looking for somebody else to boss around. This must be how Ben Franklin and the rest of the Founding Fathers felt about King George.

Teddy and I fold up the table and start down the hall. That's when things get crazy.

I hear Chad's voice from around the corner:

And then another voice:

Chad again:

I have no idea what's going on, but I hear footsteps coming our way. FAST footsteps.

We round the corner and finally I see what's happening. Randy just grabbed Chad's notebook. He's running this way. And he doesn't see us.

The table hits the floor. So does Randy. I see a flash of red on his face. Blood starts pouring from his nose.

This is awesome.

Randy doesn't hesitate. He looks right at Ms. Clarke, points at me . . . and lies through his teeth.

WHAT??? I open my mouth to protest, but Ms. Clarke speaks first.

THAT'S NOT WHAT **I** SAW.

"It looked to ME," she says, "like you gave yourSELF a bloody nose because you were running in the hall."

NATE WAS JUST MOVING A TABLE.

Randy looks stunned. Repeat: This . . . is . . . AWESOME!

GO SEE THE NURSE ABOUT THAT NOSE.

...AND AFTER SCHOOL, YOU MAY **WALK** TO THE DETENTION ROOM.

Randy hesitates. Finally he turns to go. He glares at me as he brushes by, muttering something under his breath.

"What'd he say?" Teddy asks.

"I'm not sure," I answer. "Something about . . ."

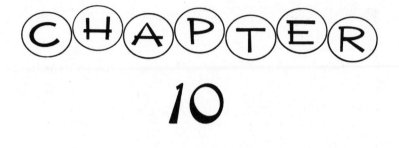

CHAPTER 10

Tomorrow's here already.

Bring it on. A winner-take-all game for the Spoffy?

"Oh, we're prepared, all right," I answer confidently.

There's a pause. Dad's looking at me like I've got two heads.

"Fleeceball, obviously. What are YOU talking about?"

He raises an eyebrow. "Your big social studies project . . . OBVIOUSLY."

 That's weird. Dad's usually clueless about what's going on at school. Now he wants to be Joe Details?

I don't really want him finding out about the deal I made with Gina. So . . .

The guys rank on me all the way to school. But I can deal with it. Things are looking pretty good right now. Not only am I basically guaranteed an A plus for being Gina's project partner, I've pulled it off without having to do any actual WORK with her. How sweet is that?

We walk into Mrs. Godfrey's room, and suddenly it's a tension convention. Everybody's looking over their projects one last time, making sure they haven't forgotten anything. Which reminds me . . .

"What for?" she says.

Duh. Because I don't trust you, of course. It would be just like you to take my name off that thing at the last second.

"How come you put YOUR name first?" I ask.

"Are you SERIOUS?" she says fiercely.

Gina snatches it back from me. "I'LL give it to her," she growls, and makes a beeline for Mrs. Godfrey.

Gag me. Look at the way they're smiling at each other. Is this social studies or a family reunion? Just hand the stinkin' thing in, Gina.

Mrs. Godfrey starts flipping through it. Her smile slowly fades. What's THAT all about?

"Oh, dear"? Did she say "oh, dear"?

"Is—is something wrong?" Gina says. Her voice sounds a tiny bit higher than usual.

"Can you tell me about these visual aids?" Mrs. Godfrey asks.

I glance at Gina. She looks . . . well, sort of . . . PANICKY.

Mrs. Godfrey frowns. "The instructions were very clear on this matter."

Visual aids are an important part of your project. You must create them yourself. Using or borrowing images from outside sources could result in a failing grade.

Gina's eyes open wide. So do mine. Her Royal Highness forgot to read the instructions? REALLY? Hey, anybody got a camera? I want to get a picture of this.

Her whole body starts to shake.

F-FAILING GRADE?

Wow. WOW! Could it be? Could Little Miss Perfect actually get an F?

"These projects are supposed to be one hundred percent original student work," Mrs. Godfrey says sternly.

Gina looks totally destroyed. What a moment. I'm going to enjoy this. I might never get this chance again.

"And, Nate . . . ," Mrs. Godfrey says, turning to me.

Gulp. Reality check. For a minute I forgot that Gina and I are a TEAM for this stupid thing.

"Well, the two of you are PARTNERS, aren't you?" she says impatiently.

Great. Thanks a LOT, Gina. I TOLD you we should have used my . . .

I grab my Ben Franklin folder from my desk. Maybe . . . MAYBE! . . . this will undo Gina's screwup.

I can tell she's a little surprised, but she opens the folder. Gina scooches over to me.

"What are you DOING?" she whispers angrily.

". . . Because in case you haven't noticed, Gina, YOUR brilliant visual aids just earned us an F!"

Gina and I wait as Mrs. Godfrey slowly looks at each page. She's not just skimming through it. She's actually READING the stuff. Hey, that works for me. There's some quality material there. Like my latest comic:

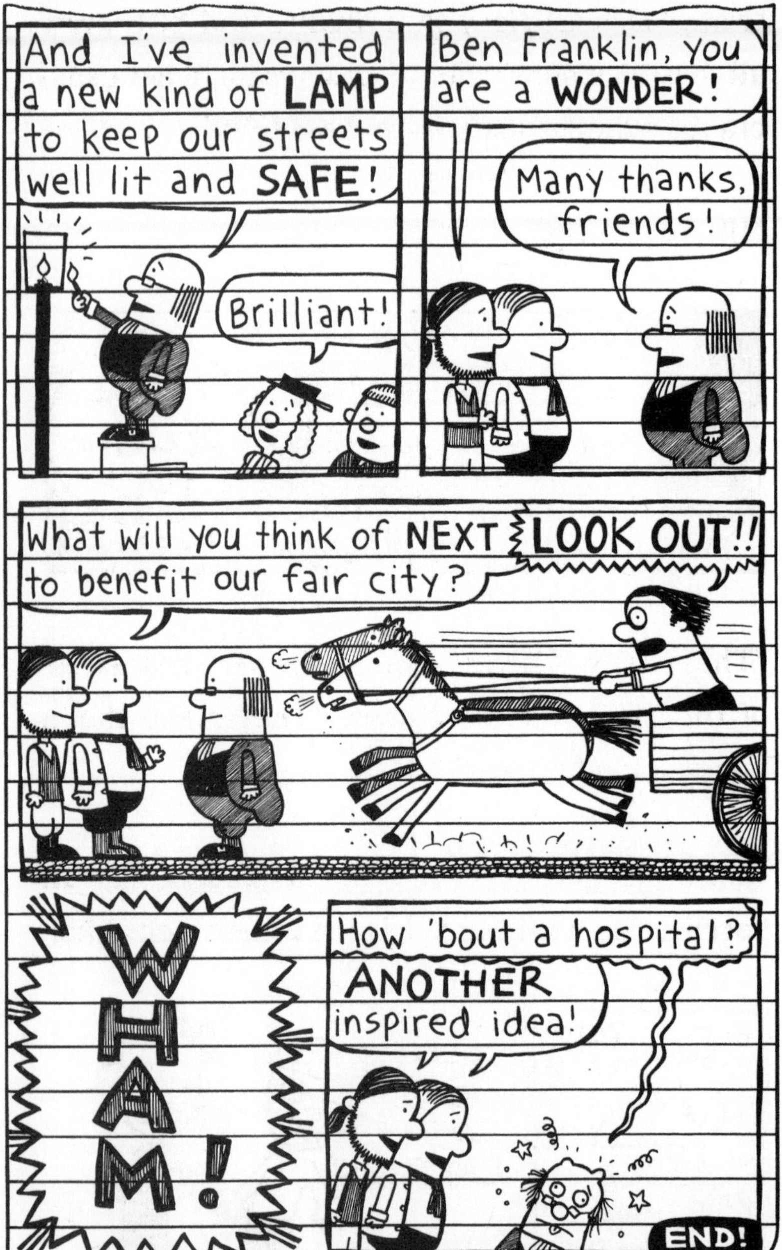
And I've invented a new kind of **LAMP** to keep our streets well lit and **SAFE**!
Brilliant!
Ben Franklin, you are a **WONDER**!
Many thanks, friends!
What will you think of **NEXT** to benefit our fair city?
LOOK OUT!!
WHAM!
How 'bout a hospital?
ANOTHER inspired idea!
END!

"Nate," Mrs. Godfrey says finally. "Did YOU draw all these cartoons?" She's not saying it in her usual crabby way. She actually looks HAPPY.

"Uh-huh," I say.

"These really ARE original, in the very best sense of the word," she continues. "They make this a one-of-a-kind project!"

Gina's losing it. Her face is all purple and she can barely talk. Is this what a heart attack looks like?

"Well, that's entirely appropriate for a Ben Franklin project," Mrs. Godfrey says. "Nate, I'm sure you can tell us why!"

For half a second I don't know what she's getting at. Then it hits me.

"He sometimes drew political cartoons and published them in his own newspaper," she explains. "And, Nate," she continues . . .

"Hear that, Gina?" I say.

Charming!

NYUK! NYUK! NYUK!

Of course Gina can't help herself. "Can we still get an A plus on the project?" she blurts out.

Mrs. Godfrey waves us back to our desks. "No promises!" she says cheerily.

BUT THANKS TO NATE'S CREATIVITY...

...THERE'S A **VERY** GOOD CHANCE!

MRS. GODFREY

We sit down. Gina's not saying anything. Hey, fine with me. I've got PLENTY to say.

"Well, Gina, despite your bonehead mistake, it sounds like you'll get your precious A plus after all," I tell her.

She turns bright red. "It wasn't all YOU!" she hisses at me. "We BOTH contributed!"

"Right, right, whatever you say. Oh, and, Gina, there's just one more thing . . ."

She looks like her face might burst into flames. I can tell she wants to scream at me, but she can't say a thing. She knows I'm right. She knows that without me, her perfect academic record would have gone straight down the toilet.

Who knew getting an A plus could be so much fun?

CHAPTER 11

You know what I hate? Waiting.

It's bad enough waiting around for everyday stuff, like the bathroom.

But when you're waiting for something really important, like our championship game against the Raptors? That's brutal. Everything moves in super slow motion.

It's only when the bell rings—FINALLY!—that time starts moving again. I fly out of the science lab, ditch my notebook, and head straight for the gym.

Randy's sort of hard to understand with his nose wrapped up like a pound of ground beef, so I'll translate. He just told me it's payback time. Guess he thinks he's got the better team.

There she is, talking to Coach. I've got to hand it to her: She promised not to play, and she hasn't. She invents a different excuse for every game.

Hm. Food poisoning. That's a new one. And today's lunch was so disgusting, it's 100 percent believable. Nice job, Gina.

But enough about her. We've got a game to win. There's only one problem:

Randy slams my very first pitch way up on the back wall. If a ball hits below the "Home of the Bobcats" banner, it's a double. If it hits above the banner, it's a home run.

Randy showboats around the bases, a huge grin on his face. When he reaches home, he jumps on the plate like he just landed on the moon or something. What a jerk.

Here's the good thing about fleeceball, though: There's a lot of scoring. Falling behind 1–0 isn't the end of the world, because you'll probably catch up. And we do. After one inning, it's 2–1, Kuddle Kittens.

If both teams continue to score at this rate, we'll win 18 to 9! Actually, make that **16** to 9, because, as the home team, we wouldn't bat in the bottom of the ninth because we blah blah blah blah blah blah blah blah...

Then it's 4–2, Raptors. Then 5–4, Kuddle Kittens. And then 6–5, Raptors. You get the idea. It's back and forth the whole game.

We reach the ninth inning tied, 9–9. And look who's up.

I hate to admit it, but Randy's a tough out. He's already gotten three hits today.

He always hits the ball hard. So it catches me a little by surprise . . .

boomp!

. . . when he dribbles a soft ground ball toward Francis at first base.

HA! Easy play. Francis scoops it up, I run over to cover the bag . . .

. . . and then it happens. Payback time.

It feels like my foot just exploded. Randy and I both hit the floor. He gets up right away, but I don't. I'm too busy rolling around in total agony.

What?? "These things happen"? Uh, yeah . . .
whenever RANDY'S around. I thought Coach was
smarter than that. Can't he see that Randy went
for my foot on PURPOSE?

Francis and Teddy help me over to the bleachers,
and Coach brings me an ice pack. "No more fleeceball for you today, Nate," he says.

"Not necessarily!" chirps Chad.

What?? Chad, are you INSANE? "NO!" I shout immediately.

Coach gives me a funny look, then turns to Gina. "Your team could use your help, Gina. Are you well enough to play?"

She stares straight at me.

"Fantastic!" says Coach.

Apparently Coach doesn't realize how UNfantastic this is. In fact, this could be a complete disaster.

"Nothing." She smirks. "Just filling in for an injured teammate."

Oh, that's a riot. "Listen, Gina . . ."

Is she serious? "Dream ON, Gina." I snort.

Before she can bite my head off, Coach interrupts. "Enough talk, you two," he says. "Let's play ball."

As Gina walks out to right field, I can hear some of the Raptors laughing. I'm starting to get a really bad feeling about this.

At first, things go okay. The Raptors load the bases, but we manage to get two outs. All we need is one more to keep the score tied.

They hit it to Gina.

11–9, Raptors. We get the third out on the next pitch, but the damage is done. Thanks, Gina.

We still have one more chance to bat. The good news is: Teddy and Francis reach base with two outs. The bad news is: Here comes out number three.

Earth to Chad: No, she can't.

See? Her stuffed cat would have a better chance of getting a hit. This is awful. I can't just sit here and watch us lose. I've got to DO something!

She's speechless. But Coach isn't.

"SIT DOWN, Nate," he barks.

He means it. I let go of the broom handle and hobble back to the bleachers. This stinks. I'm the captain of the team, but I'm stuck watching.

Here it comes: the final pitch of the game.

For a few seconds the gym is completely silent. Then . . .

"HOME RUN!" screams Chad.

I don't say anything. I'm in shock. It's not until Coach walks toward us with the Spoffy that I actually believe my eyes.

"Congratulations, Kuddle Kittens!" he says. Then he hands the trophy to . . .

What's up with THAT? She plays ONE INNING and all of a sudden she's Joe All-Star?

Oop. Hold it, she's walking over here. Maybe she realizes that the TEAM CAPTAIN should get the Spoffy. Let's hear what she's got to say for herself.

Ouch. That was cold. She struts off, holding up the Spoffy like she's the Statue of Liberty. "What an amazing game!" I hear Chad tell her.

CHAPTER 12

Poor Nate's **SPORTS WRAP**

KUDDLE KITTENS WIN SPOFFY

Led by team captain *NATE WRIGHT,* the Kuddle Kittens (<u>real</u> name: Psycho Dogs) beat Randy Betancourt's Raptors in yesterday's fleeceball champion-ship, 12-11. A lucky hit in the ninth inning enabled the Kuddle Kittens to come back from a 2-run deficit

"LUCKY HIT?"

I spin around. Gina's reading over my shoulder.
Can't a literary genius write in peace?

"You just hate that I saved us from losing!" she
snarls.

"Oh, really?" I ask her.

"That was DIFFERENT!" she says, her voice rising.
"I did the REAL work!"

"My comics aren't stupid, Gina," I shoot back at her, "which you'd KNOW if you'd spent a little time STUDYING them!"

"Wha . . . ? STUDYING?" she sputters. "Who are YOU to lecture ME about STUDYING?"

YOU KNOW NOTHING ABOUT STUDYING! YOU'VE NEVER STUDIED A DAY IN YOUR LIFE!!

"Shouting is not permitted in the library, Gina," Mrs. Hickson says. She pulls out a little pink pad.

Gina gasps. "The—the detention room?"

"It's across the hall from the faculty lounge," I say helpfully.

She points at me, looking totally outraged. "YOU'RE the one who should go to detention!"

"Stop comparing yourself to Ben Franklin!" she hisses at me.

Oh, I don't know about that. Ben and I have a lot in common. I'll bet if he were alive today, he and I would get along pretty well.

I think he'd get a real charge out of me.

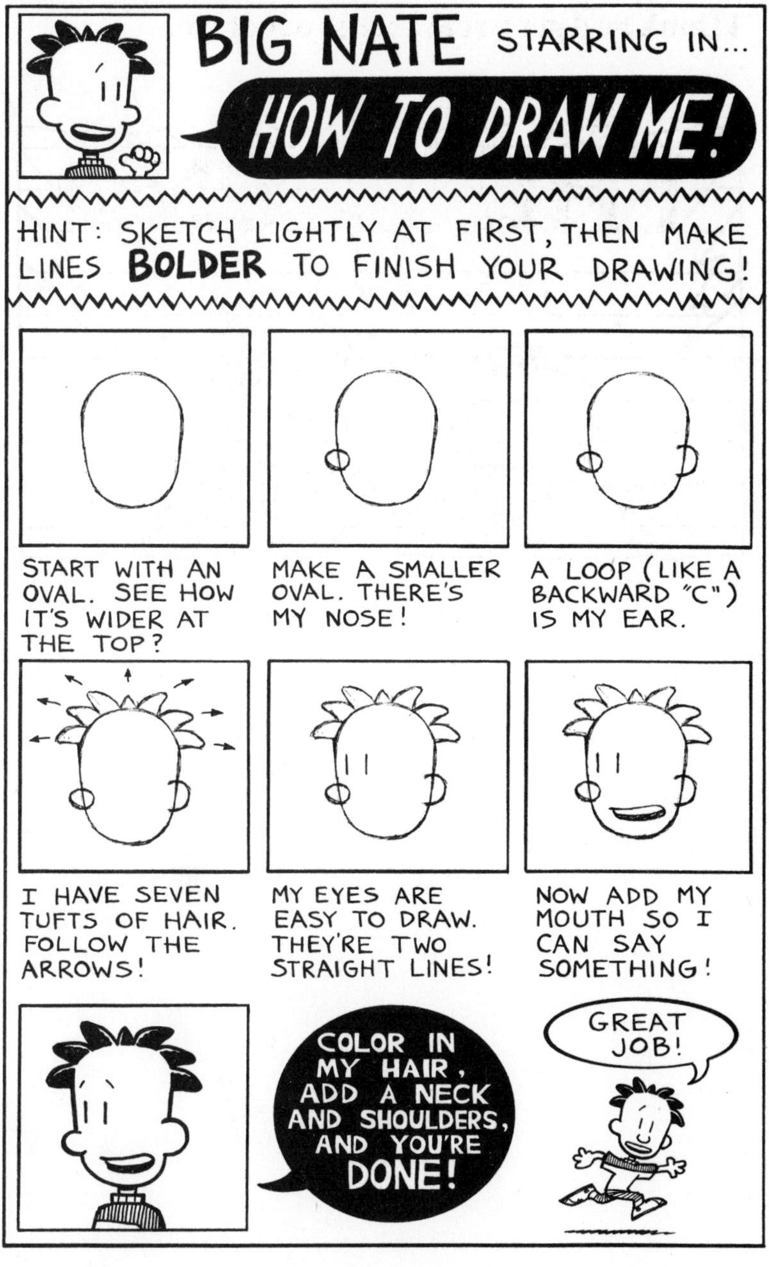
BIG NATE STARRING IN...
HOW TO DRAW ME!
HINT: SKETCH LIGHTLY AT FIRST, THEN MAKE LINES BOLDER TO FINISH YOUR DRAWING!
START WITH AN OVAL. SEE HOW IT'S WIDER AT THE TOP?
MAKE A SMALLER OVAL. THERE'S MY NOSE!
A LOOP (LIKE A BACKWARD "C") IS MY EAR.
I HAVE SEVEN TUFTS OF HAIR. FOLLOW THE ARROWS!
MY EYES ARE EASY TO DRAW. THEY'RE TWO STRAIGHT LINES!
NOW ADD MY MOUTH SO I CAN SAY SOMETHING!
COLOR IN MY HAIR, ADD A NECK AND SHOULDERS, AND YOU'RE DONE!
GREAT JOB!

READ ALL THE Big NATE BOOKS TODAY!

NOVELS

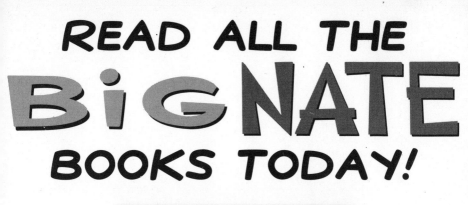

READ ALL THE BiG NATE BOOKS TODAY!

ACTIVITY BOOKS

COMIC COMPILATIONS